MW01625009

The Haunted Reckoning

MICHELLE DOREY

The Haunted Ones 5
Paranormal Suspense

Copyright © 2019 Michelle Dorey
All rights reserved.
ISBN: 978-1-988913-16-2
Monarch Moments
Cover Design by Juan Padron
https://www.instagram.com/padrondesign/
Edited by Paula Grundy
https://paulaproofreader.wixsite.com/home

101219PRT

CONTENTS

ONE

Cory knew he was early to pick up his daughter, but he had to find out what his skanky ex was up to. He started the truck and blasted the heater to get the chill out of his bones. After sitting there for the better part of an hour, he was rewarded when the kitchen light in the small house across the street blazed. He could finally see the bitch.

She stood at the sink, her jet black hair flowing over her shoulders as she turned slightly, her lips moving as she talked. She hadn't changed from the work uniform even though she'd been home for a couple of hours.

His eyes narrowed while his hands tightened on the steering wheel. She was nothing but a two-bit hustler from El Salvador. She should have counted her blessings that he'd married her to get her out of that shithole country. Instead the bitch had him arrested for assault and even got a restraining order so he couldn't see his own kid.

He snorted. With his daughter's dark eyes and hair, the total Latino complexion, who knew if she really *was* his kid? His blond hair and fair skin was absent in Aubree. He wouldn't put anything past his skanky ex-wife to screw around on him.

Which was probably what she was planning to do as soon

as he left with Aubree. No doubt she was waiting to get showered and changed into sexy clothes for some jerk she'd picked up somewhere. He could feel the vein in his temple pulse, his teeth crackling as he ground them.

Screw it!

He got out of the truck and crossed the narrow street. Even the neighborhood was seedy and what his father would term "starter or retirement" homes. She'd left their extended ranch for *this*? What a loser.

After rapping on the door, he heard movement and Noele's voice calling their daughter in from the backyard. That was another thing! She'd let a six-year-old kid play outside, and it was getting dark! He should have pressed for full custody when he'd taken her to court. He probably could have gotten it with that hotshot lawyer he'd hired. His mistake was just settling on extended visitation rights.

The door opened, and she stood there, barely hiding her contempt in the tight line of her lips and eyes that looked right through him.

"You're early. You aren't supposed to be here until five. Aubree isn't ready, and I still have to pack her bag."

"Sorry." It sounded as insincere as his plastic smile. "Can I come in and wait? It's chilly outside, Noele."

She rolled her eyes and sighed. "You can stay in the foyer." Without another word she spun and walked through the laundry room to call to Aubree from the backyard.

He hated the fact that he checked out her ass as she walked away, but he couldn't help himself. It was the thing that had first attracted him, and he wasn't immune even after...what, seven years?

Seeing the sway of her hips, the still-tiny waist and uniform that clung to every curve and swell of her figure, he felt a familiar stirring. Damn it! And she was probably going to be sharing that booty with some low-life later that night. His heart beat faster, and he could feel his blood boil.

Her voice had that zesty Latino lilt when she called from the kitchen. "Make sure she goes to bed at eight, and have her back by ten tomorrow morning. I work noon to eight, and I want to see her before I leave her with Mrs. Noonan."

"Hey! Why not let me keep her till you're off? I'll bring her back tomorrow evening." He made his voice sound upbeat. It sounded phony even to his own ears. The kid would drive him bonkers, but it was worth it if that would piss Noele off.

She poked her head around the corner, giving him "the look", lips twisted in scorn to go along with the eye roll.

It had always made him see red, and today wasn't any different. "I have that right, you know! I won in court if you recall. Aubree can stay with me for forty-eight hours, and you've got nothing to say about it. Especially if you're not even here, pawning her off on a babysitter!"

"Gilipollas de mierda!" She switched to English, losing the deafening pitch. "You shouldn't be anywhere *near* Aubree! And so help me God, if you hurt her, I'll—"

His hand shot out before he knew it! The blow caught her on the side of her head, knocking her to the floor. He was about to follow up with another when movement from the doorway down the hall caught his eye.

Aubree stood there, in her red plaid coat, her thumbnail between her tiny teeth while her eyes were wide, staring at him in terror.

"Go outside, Aubree! Now!"

At Noele's words, Aubree spun around and disappeared into the laundry room. The door to the outside slammed shut behind her.

In a flash, Cory was right on her tail. When he stepped out of the doorway she was across the yard, standing next to her sandbox. He called to her. "Aubree. Come here. I'm not going to hurt you." She clutched at the buttons of the red plaid coat, and instead, backed away.

"I said, come here!" Cory raced across the yard and scooped her up. Her small arms beat at his chest while she squirmed, trying to kick him with her feet. This was his daughter! Trying to hurt him and get away from him!

He slammed the door after him and strode into the kitchen.

Noele had gotten back on her feet and screamed when she saw Aubree pinned in the crook of his arm.

"Leave her alone! I'll call the cops! Put her down!"

He smiled and let Aubree slip lower, setting her down on her feet while his hands cupped her small shoulders. There was satisfaction in Noele's terror seeing him hurt her daughter. His hands lifted higher, fingers circling the tiny neck which he could snap like a pencil if he wanted. He brushed the child's shoulders. "Nice coat. The red plaid looks good on you." He looked up to Noele, his eyes filled with hate. "Brand new too. How'd you afford it? Got another job *serving the public*? You working at a strip club or something?"

Noele lunged at him, reaching for Aubree while clawing at him trying to gouge his eye. But he was too fast; his fist caught her jaw, knocking her back on her ass.

Blood poured from her mouth as she shook her head. Despite being dazed from the blow she was already trying to get up again. In one fell swoop he gripped Aubree with one hand while his foot planted on Noele's chest pinning her to the floor.

It was a macabre dance as Cory's foot pinned Noele's struggling form as he strangled the child. His grip tightened around Aubree's neck, impervious to her frantic beating at his arms, her feet kicking his leg. All the while Noele lashed out, trying desperately to escape his hold on her chest, begging him to stop. It was rewarding watching her desperation. Served the bitch right.

It ended way too soon. Aubree became heavier in his hands. He let go of her. The small lifeless body slumped onto the floor. The best part of it was the anguish and screams from Noele watching her daughter die.

His chest filled and he became lighter. The fun wasn't over. Noele's pretty face would hardly be recognizable in the morgue. Lifting his foot, he bent over Nicole and moved in with his fists…

TWO

"You couldn't have known, Paige. These things... well, sometimes bad, monstrous things happen. Who knows why?" Sheila's eyes glistened with tears for her friend.

Once more Paige's gaze was drawn to the photo in the newspaper. The dark-haired mother's eyes accused her while the little girl's were...

Her eyes squeezed shut. Oh God, this couldn't be happening! This couldn't be true. Yet there it was in black, white, and living color screaming condemnation and horror. They were dead, brutally murdered, and she was to blame.

"Sheila's right," Bradley said. He looked at the two women, sitting across from him on the leather sofa, in his office. "You did your job exactly as you were supposed to. You defended his right to custody to the best of your ability and knowledge. You aren't responsible that in a fit of anger... hell... rage, that he *snapped.* That was his fault, not yours."

His voice and words barely registered in Paige's brain. Her thoughts were on Cory Smith. He'd seemed so damn genuine in his desire to raise his daughter. He'd even broke down in tears at the prospect that he'd only see her once a month in supervised visits. Well, Paige took care of that wrinkle and got him full access with limited restrictions.

And now they were dead. Great job, Paige.

How could he have done this? There had to be a mistake. Some thug must have broken into the house and...

Her voice cracked when she looked up at her boss and mentor, Bradley Peterson. "The police think he killed them. Is there evidence? You read the article. I haven't had time yet to—"

"They discovered the bodies yesterday afternoon." Sheila eased closer to her on the sofa, placing her hand over Paige's clasped fingers, "When the wife failed to show up at work for a second day, and there were no answers to their phone calls, they sent someone over. Her car was at the house, but she didn't answer the door. Of course, they notified the police and..."

"But it could have been someone breaking in. Some thief or drug addict who killed them." But even as Paige said it—a desperate attempt to absolve her own guilt in this horror—she knew in her bones that wasn't the way it went down.

Bradley pushed away from the desk and sighed, "No, they're pretty sure the husband did it. When I saw the article, I called a friend at headquarters. They checked where Cory worked, and he didn't show up for work Friday night or on the weekend. It corresponds to their estimated time of death: Friday afternoon."

Paige sank lower into the sofa, no longer able to harbor a glimmer of hope. Of course, as the senior partner, he would call the police to learn more. His law firm had represented Cory Smith in the custody battle against the now deceased wife. The police were bound to contact the firm, so Bradley took the proactive step.

He pressed a button on his phone. "Cancel Sheila and Paige's appointments today, Beth."

Paige looked over at Bradley. He looked years older than sixty-one as he leaned back in his office chair. He might be all business, looking out for the firm's welfare, but deep inside, contrary to popular opinion about attorneys, he was a deeply caring man.

This was a tragedy they all had played a part in despite their protestations that no one could have foreseen this. Thanks to Paige's skill in representing Cory, she'd given him the access he needed to do this. Up until that time, Noele Smith had been safe with a restraining order keeping her ex from any contact. Paige, with all the skill of an experienced trial lawyer, had driven a Mack truck through the gaping holes in the evidence supporting that order.

"Come on, Paige." Sheila rose to her feet, "I'll drive you home and stay with you for a while. This is a tough thing to deal with." She shot a look at Bradley, who nodded.

Paige looked up at her, feeling the hot sting of tears behind her eyes. She took a deep breath, forcing her voice to answer. "Worse for Noele and Aubree though. Jesus. How could I—"

Bradley leaned forward, staring at his clasped . "Take a few days off, Paige." He sighed and looked up at her. "This is the law, and your job is to make sure that your client receives the fullest protection under it." He glanced away, his voice gentle. "Sometimes it's not really about justice, but it's always making damn sure the rules get followed, and that's exactly what you did." He looked back to Paige. "It's a shitty thing to happen so early in your career...but sooner or later you were bound to have an episode like this."

"It makes me question everything!" she said in a hushed voice.

"Yeah, I know." He shook his head slowly. "I wish you had had more seasoning before this happened, but it is what it is."

"I hate that phrase..."

"Yeah, but it really applies here. There's nothing more to do but accept that it happened, and it was beyond your control. There really isn't any alternative, is there?"

Paige shrugged.

"Yeah, I understand. You just took a hell of a punch to the gut." Now his eyes took on his "boss man" look. "Take a few days if you have to, but you'll survive. You'll be a better lawyer for it." He took a case folder from the pile on the left and opened it, signaling the meeting was over.

Paige swayed slightly when she got to her feet. The room felt askew as she trudged after Sheila. This was a nightmare that she'd never wake up from. Two people were dead! An innocent child, barely six years old. A mother trying desperately to protect her daughter in a system where the game was rigged. Cory had the cash to hire the best representation while Noele had been represented by legal aid. No way could she have won.

And it cost them their lives.

THREE

Paige was still stiff from shock as she stepped out of the car. The walkway leading up to the townhouse, was littered with leaves from the recent windstorm, and she'd have to rake them up soon. The leaf cleanup from the city was in a couple of weeks and...

Damn! A fresh flood of tears filled her eyes, picturing the photos in the newspaper. It was the little girl's face that set it off, so fresh and open. It was a school picture, from some professional outfit, replete with a set of giant crayons in the background. Dark wisps of hair framed her round cheeks, her mouth curved in a smile, and her brown eyes danced like a sprite. You could see from the photo she was a lovely, intelligent and feisty little girl. Just like in real life.

But not anymore! Another sob escaped her throat, and more followed. She paused with the key in the lock, unable to turn it as her shoulders heaved.

"Here…let me." Sheila nudged Paige's hand away and then pushed the door wide open. She pulled Paige closer, her arm draped over the younger woman's shoulders. "Come on, Paige. I'll make us some tea. Me mum always said there's no problem that a nice cuppa wouldn't solve."

Paige stepped into the house and toed off her shoes. But Sheila's mother never killed anyone though, did she? No, that was Paige's specialty.

Okay, maybe she hadn't *directly* killed anyone. But she sure as hell had enabled it to happen. What were the charges for an act like that? Manslaughter? Second degree?

Christ! Listen to her. A mother and child were dead, and here she was feeling sorry for herself!

She let Sheila lead her into the kitchen and set her down on the chair. A flash of Cory broke through the fog of her brain. He'd been so damn polite and heartwarmingly earnest in his proclaimed love of his daughter. Hell, he'd even managed to speak well of his ex, never blaming her for being so protective of Aubree. Noele had been a good mother, although she had a tendency to hover over their child. But she was from El Salvador and that was probably their way, according to Cory.

Sheila took a seat across from her and pressed a tissue into her hand. "Cry, Paige. Get it out of your system. I'm here for you, girl. Take as long as you need."

Paige nodded. She noticed steam drifting out of the spout of the teakettle and rose to her feet. Her legs felt wooden as she stepped over to the cabinet and pulled out a bottle of red wine. She grabbed a water glass and filled it to the brim. With a wan smile, she glanced over at Sheila. "Sorry. Tea isn't going to cut it."

"You do what you have to. My mum's remedy was tea, but the Irish reprobate who was my father swore by whiskey. This is a day to just get through, Paige. You'll do that. This is a tough one." She ran her finger through shaggy blonde locks of hair and looked up at the ceiling silently for a moment.

"I had a case similar to this one, once." Her smile became lopsided. "It didn't end in death but it could have. My client was a tough lady. She knew her ex, and she was prepared to deal with it when he lost. He'll carry a scar on his face for the rest of his life, thanks to his bullying ways." She got up and poured water into the teapot, her words low and soothing, "You just never know about people, Paige: what they're capable of...good and bad."

Paige took a long sip of the wine and wiped her lips with the back of her hand. "But that's just it, Sheila. I should have known. There had to have been some hint as to what he really wanted...who he was. How did he slip under my radar?"

Sheila looked up from stirring milk into her mug of tea. "Some people are cold. They can hide their true nature under a veneer of normal. Or maybe, as Brad said, he just snapped. Maybe the wife said something, looked at him the wrong way, and"—she snapped her fingers—"they're dead."

It was small consolation but she'd take it. Anything to ease the heavy mantle of guilt from her shoulders. Maybe it hadn't been premeditated. Maybe when he'd dropped off Aubree, the wife said something to set him off.

Her stomach clenched tighter, feeling the wine rise to the back of her throat. But why murder his daughter? The wife...sure, that could happen. Men give into rage every day and wives suffer for it. As heinous as it it, it happens far too often. She shuddered at that thought.

But it takes a special kind of evil to murder your own child.

FOUR

"Stay the hell down! The cops are lookin' for you, for shit's sake! I'm not going to be caught aiding and abetting a criminal, Bucko."

Cory stared up into the rearview mirror, locking eyes with his father. As usual, the old man was more interested in looking out for his own welfare rather than Cory's. His eyes narrowed as he hunkered lower in the back seat of the Escalade. If there were any other way out of this mess, he'd jump at it, but the old man was all he had. It rankled to be under his father's thumb...again.

Well, not completely under the old prick's thumb. Thanks to that little tidbit he'd picked up when he was fourteen, seeing his father with the hooker and then reading about her death the next day had been a gold nugget. He'd been able to hold it over him and leverage it to some extent. Real providential, that evening had been.

His leg knotted up in a cramp, but the discomfort in his bladder was worse. "How much farther? I gotta take a leak."

Michael glanced back at his son and sneered. "You hold on, Bucko. Think I care about that? You're lucky I've got a place to stash you. You just hole up there for a while and then get the hell outta Dodge, y'hear? Grow a beard if you're capable. You might want to change your hair color too."

Cory bristled at his father's words. Even though he was thirty, never asking for a penny from the old bastard, the old man still treated him like a punk. He held his tongue though. He graduated from his father's school of hard knocks years ago and wasn't about to take any remedial classes. The old guy could still probably beat the hell out of him; God knows he's had the practice.

"Don't worry. As soon as the heat dies down a bit, I'm outta here. Maybe I'll go west and pop in on dear old Mom. Shall I give her your regards?" Cory's lips twitched. That last bit would sting. Mom had taken off as soon as he finished high school and Dad never got over it. Mom up and leaving him—especially with nothing to go to. She'd left an affluent lifestyle, for what? A minimum wage secretarial job in some two-bit insurance office? It wasn't that his father missed her. Mom had been like the Rolex on the old man's wrist, *his*. She wasn't just the old man's wife, she *belonged* to him!

Just like Noele and Aubree. Damn her to hell. He sneered. Hell. That's just where the two of them probably were right now. He couldn't hurt that bitch enough. But choking the life out of Aubree right in front of her? Now *that* had been fun.

Bitch. Who did she think she was? Some two-bit whore from El Salvador. Sure, he hadn't been rich but at least she'd never had to eat dog meat. The nerve of the woman getting a restraining order against him. All he'd ever done was give the kid a light tap on her arm. He'd showed that bitch though. Thanks to the fancy-pants lawyer, her restraining order and custody got shot out of the water.

He was jolted back to the here and now by the jostle of the car hitting a pothole. He squeezed his legs together to keep from wetting himself. "Seriously. Where is this place, *Alaska*?"

"Shut up. We have a bit more to go, okay? You'll have the comforts of home, almost." The old man chuckled. "Less a wife and child though, thanks to your temper. How many times did I tell you about that? You've got to push it down, the craving. Or at least if you can't do that, channel it."

Cory's eyes narrowed when he parried, "Like you did with Mary-Jane Harrow? Pick up a skanky whore and beat her till she was dead? That's your forte isn't it, Dad? Sorry, but there's not that many streetwalkers where I live."

"Where you *lived*, son. That life is over. And so is any more contact with me."

For a moment Cory froze, but then his words came out in a rush. "What? What about me? I'm going to be in some cabin in the middle of nowhere. You've got to help me. Bring me food at least. How will I survive?"

The short laugh that burst from his father's mouth sent a spike of rage through Cory.

"You were never one for foresight, were you? Even back when you were only twelve... How many neighbors lost their cats? You never thought they'd wonder about you skulking around after dark?" The old man blew a fast sigh. "*Of course* I'll see that you have food. I bought you that phone, but you're not to call me—only when absolutely necessary. The police are probably watching my home and office."

Cory's face tightened. "So how you gonna do that? Get supplies to me, I mean."

"I'll leave them in a duffel bag at the edge of the property. I don't have to even stop the car to do that." He looked in the rearview mirror and their eyes met. "I'll show you where when we get there. You just keep to the cabin. The old biddy who owns it hardly even knows her last name. I've kept the electricity on, and there's a woodstove and a well. It's actually kind of nice. I was thinking of buying it. Build some more cabins and make a fortune. There're almost ten acres of waterfront property."

Cory decided to throw the old man a bone. "Now you're sounding like the successful Realtor you are. No wonder you make so much money." The old biddy wouldn't be the first client his father had taken advantage of. He'd heard the rumors about that family who were forced out of their home when the father was killed in a car accident. Funny how Dad's firm was the Realtor of the new subdivision that went up there. Hmm. Yeah, real funny coincidence.

"I'd say the fact you never came near me...well after the *incident* a few years ago, was a blessing in disguise. Every one of my neighbors will attest to the fact that we were estranged." His father eased up on the gas and turned the steering wheel.

Cory risked sitting higher. The vehicle's headlights showed a dirt track bordered by tree growth so dense, it looked like they were heading down a tunnel.

The vehicle stopped, and his father pointed to a wooden sign. *Sanctuary* was painted on the rough piece of wood in red letters. Corny. "Right there, see? I'll leave a duffel bag with provisions a few feet from that sign. The cabin's about five hundred feet around a bend. You'd never see it from the road. Not that there's much traffic up here anyway. The nearest cabin is half a mile away. They shut it down for the season, so no one will be around."

Cory edged forward on the seat, looking past his father out the windshield. Right on time, a rustic log cabin was highlighted in the beam.

Home sweet home. For now.

FIVE

Paige awoke with a start. Her forehead was pimpled with tiny beads of sweat, and her heart thudded hard. She clutched her pillow like a teddy bear, panting. Gradually her breathing evened out.

It was just a dream. But even so, her eyes darted around the room trying to ground herself in the familiar comforts. It was that little girl. She dreamed of her—watching her play in a small fenced area, jumping from a tire swing onto the ground, racing to a small wooden sandbox. It had been so real!

The worst of it was the sense of dread that infused her peering at the girl playing in the sand. Something bad was about to happen, and she had to get the kid out of there. When the girl had looked up, gazing past her, the smile on her face morphed into fear. Her eyes grew wider, and she sprung back, backing up till she was stopped by the fence. Her scream still rang in Paige's ears.

Aubree.

Of course, it was understandable that she'd dreamed of the little girl. Her death and the woman whom she'd watched in the courtroom testifying against her ex-husband were bound to play out in her dreams.

Her eyes closed, and for the hundredth time, she wished that she had believed the woman rather than arguing for her client's case. That monster, Cory Smith, had done it. The police thought so, and so did she. They'd find him, and when they did, she'd make it a point to pay him a visit in his prison cell.

She glanced at the clock on her bedside table. The red numbers glowing in the dark showed it was just ten minutes after three in the morning. The dull ache in her temples was the result of killing practically a whole bottle of wine. She'd hoped to numb her mind to escape the guilt, but it was now tomorrow and the guilt was still there. Even worse.

Throwing the covers back she eased out of bed and stumbled across the room, drawn by the night-light's amber glow in the bathroom. She flipped the switch and found a bottle of aspirin in the medicine cabinet. With a quick toss of her hand, she dry-swallowed them. A glance in the mirror showed dark cusps under her eyes while her hair hung in strings over her shoulders.

She scooped a handful of water from the tap to clear the foul taste from her mouth. As she was about to hit the light switch she gasped. A face had appeared in the mirror behind her! She spun around but there was nothing—only the wall with a shelf of toiletries showed.

But something had been there. Her heartbeat raced, pulsing in her ears. Not just *something.* It had been a face: a little girl with dark hair and wide eyes.

Giving her head a shake, she flipped the light switch off. There was nothing there now. Her mind, wallowing in despair, had not only caused the nightmare but was now messing with her vision. She was tired, and if truth be known, also hung-over. She'd get a few hours more of sleep and face the day later. There was no way she was going to work. Bradley had suggested she take time off, and as usual, he was right. Just a few days, and she'd be able to get back to the office.

She hoped.

***

Six hours later, Paige sighed opening her eyes to the bright fall sunshine pouring into her bedroom window. Bone weary, she pushed herself from the warmth of the bed and trudged past the living room and entered the kitchen. Her laptop sat on the table where she'd left it the night before. After clicking the button on the coffeemaker, she took a seat at the table to boot her email up.

There was one from Sheila as well as one from Beth. She'd read those later. Like a moth drawn to a flame, she opened the news app to see if there was anything new on the Smith homicide. With any luck, they'd caught the creep—her client.

It was a blow to her gut when Cory's face stared back at her from the front page. She peered at his picture, seeking any clues in his eyes, or the tight set of his lips, anything that she'd never picked up on before. Was it her imagination or was there a sense of "deadness" in his pale blue eyes? It was like gazing at the eye of a fish tucked in ice at the supermarket. Why had she never noticed that before? This photo looked recent, probably from a family album. The folds of the hood of his sweater nestled around his neck.

If she was right and it was a family photo, then whoever took the shot had captured a glimpse of his soul. With the thin lips and dead eyes, the expression reflected was blank and cold. She could see what he'd always kept guarded, projecting an affable politeness to the world.

Or maybe she was reading too much into one picture, making it fit with what she now knew.

She got up and poured a mug of coffee before returning to read what was written earlier that morning.

> *The bodies of Noele Smith and her six-year-old daughter, Aubree, were found at around 2 p.m. October 13. The coroner's report shows that both deaths occurred on or around Friday afternoon. Noele Smith died from multiple blows to her head while the child's death occurred as a result of strangulation.*

Police are asking for the public's help in locating the ex-husband and father of the deceased. He is wanted for questioning in this matter. Cory Smith, employed as a bouncer for a local bar, Blue Beered, failed to show up for his shift Friday night and has not been seen by friends or co-workers since.

Paige sat back and sighed. There was a call that she'd have to make later that morning. Bradley may have bought her a day in talking to the homicide investigators, but she knew that they'd also want to hear from her. It wasn't something she looked forward to. She felt guilty enough without some damn detective raking her over the coals.

But maybe she deserved it. She'd dropped the ball and given this maniac access to his wife and child.

She should have known.

She gulped half the coffee down and reached for her cell phone. It was time to grow a spine and face this.

SIX

Paige left the police station tugging her leather jacket tighter to her neck. The breeze had picked up in the two hours she'd spent with the two detectives. If she'd had any thought that they were going to go a bit easier on her those hopes were quickly dashed.

This wasn't a large city, and heinous crimes such as this were rare. Added to that was the fact that Noele had barely been recognizable after being beaten so badly. Plus, the child was so young and innocent, the police were totally pissed. The whole city was. This was Albany, not Chicago or Detroit.

She had to get her car from the office. She had her own spot in the lot and figured walking to the police station would help with her hangover. It did; she arrived a lot more clearheaded.

Heading back, she replayed the interview with the detective over in her mind. Peterson wouldn't even talk with her at his desk! Instead, he put her in an interview room like a common suspect!

"New procedures," he'd said with a sneer. Bullshit. He wanted her to know loud and clear what he thought of her. They may both work for the justice system, but she was on the wrong side on this one.

The way he grilled her—it got real clear, real fast that Peterson blamed her for the murders.

She let out a sigh. *'That makes two of us.'* She hugged herself as a gust of cold wind rolled over her, put her head down and kept on going. Parking ten blocks away didn't feel like such a great idea anymore.

After walking for ten minutes or so, the sounds of children's laughter and squeals yanked her back to reality.

There was a park that she could cut through to save a few minutes getting to her car. A group of women, young mothers bundled in jackets, chatted as their children tired themselves playing on the climbers and swings. Many of the women looked to be her age; some were close to thirty, enjoying their children's preschool years. Others were more like her, well past the "dirty-thirty" birthday, but still young enough to enjoy their kids.

For a few moments, Paige paused, deliberating on whether to take the shortcut. Not only was it a reminder of the gruesome murder, but there was that personal element. She'd purposely postponed marriage and a family until she was established, career-wise. She had determined at an early age to *not* follow in her mother's footsteps.

It was funny sometimes. The very lifestyle her mother chose in raising her single-handedly had caused Paige to feel like an outsider a lot of the time. Her friends all had dads or stepdads at least. Now here she was eschewing that kind of life and still feeling like an outsider next to these young mothers with toddlers tugging at their jackets.

'Enough with the self-pity, Paige. This isn't all about you.' She turned, striding down the walkway that ran through the park. She forced a chuckle down at the next thought. *'Sure it is. You're always the star in your own life. Duh.'*

She looked over at the children as she passed by the circular space of equipment. One little guy yelled at his mother to look as he dangled from a bar on the jungle gym, waving his hands while his legs hooked around the iron. Another child in a green hoodie was clambering up the side, trying to make his way to the top.

Her gaze drifted past the monkey bars to a set of swings where a dark-haired little girl, in a red plaid coat sat. No smile, but it was her brown eyes staring back that riveted her attention.

Aubree? Paige tripped on a crack in the walk and she stumbled, catching herself.

When she looked back the girl was gone. The swing she had been sitting on was perfectly still. Paige came to a full stop, searching the area around it for where the girl had gone. Her heart beat faster in her chest as she peered at the empty border of lawn littered with fallen leaves. Worse yet was the unreal sense inside her mind!

Had she actually *seen* a girl on the swing? She couldn't have disappeared so fast. And she'd looked exactly like Aubree? But...but that couldn't be.

Oh God. She was seeing things, *again.* Last night in the mirror and now in broad daylight? This was affecting her more than she'd thought possible.

"Can I help you? Did you lose your kid?"

She spun around at the woman's voice behind her. A black woman, her lips the same shade as her crimson jacket stood gaping at her.

"N...no. I thought I saw someone I know." She felt her face grow hot under the woman's piercing gaze. "It was just a coincidence, I guess." She hurried on, unwilling to further any contact with the woman. She was probably watching for any threat to her child playing there. A strange woman sizing up the play area would be someone to keep an eye on.

Her sneakers crunched leaves as she hurried away, her mind frenzied. Images of that poor, poor little girl ran through her imagination like a slideshow. Aubree as a newborn, her first steps, her first birthday. One image after another of that child's face invaded Paige's mind. Try as she might to change her thoughts—a grocery list, her dinner, the cases on her desk—anything but Aubree. In spite of her efforts, the child's face peeked through, overwhelming any other thoughts.

Why? She'd never met the child! Noele had been the one at the hearing. If anything you'd think the mother's face would be the one she'd see with her mind's eye. She'd questioned the woman. Hell, she'd even grilled her. This didn't make sense.

But then. Neither did murdering a mother and child.

SEVEN

Cory rummaged around in the forest surrounding the cabin looking for downed trees and branches. The cabin had a small electric heater, but without insulation, the cold had crept in through the windows and walls. Twice he'd woken up shivering and piling on more mothball-smelling blankets. Dad had said the owner was elderly, and from the smell in the cabin, it had to be true. Everything he touched had that "old people" smell.

Tonight he'd get a fire going in that cast-iron stove. With any luck, it would burn through the night, and the cold outside wouldn't matter. He spotted a large branch as thick as his thigh laying in a thicket of brush and made his way over. He grabbed it and began dragging it back to the cabin where there was a Swede saw to cut it into smaller pieces. He'd barely dislodged it from the overgrown vegetation when a streak of gray darted out from under it.

At the chittering sound, his head turned to see a striped animal snarling at him. A raccoon with bristled fur, its black eyes watching him, stood its ground. The thing was much bigger than a cat, even the old toms that he'd tormented as a kid.

"Git!" He lunged at the animal, his feet thudding hard against the forest floor.

Still, the animal held its turf, chattering and cursing at him. Only a few feet from his foot, it was so close he could see the brown on its teeth, see its whiskers twitch. He eyed the raccoon silently. There had to be a reason that it wasn't running away. He'd obviously disturbed its home.

Babies! It was like a light bulb went off in his head.

He shoved the branch to the side and then turned to the jumble of leaves and brush that lay in a mound. What he'd taken as bushes he could now see was the crafted home of this creature, camouflaged in the foliage. After a quick glance at the mother raccoon, he stepped closer to the mound and let fly with his foot, kicking sticks and leaves everywhere.

A searing pain in his other ankle made him yelp. He almost fell, stumbling back. The raccoon clung to his pants, its claws hooked into the tough denim. He beat at it with his fists and his other leg gave it a swift boot, knocking it off. It rolled but then came to its feet. The striped little ninja was ready for more, defending its litter.

His ankle throbbed, and he could feel wet warmth ooze over his foot inside the sneaker. Shit! The little fucker had bitten him and now he was bleeding! He'd probably get rabies or some other horrible disease.

"Okay! I'm going. We'll call it a draw." He backed away slowly never taking his eyes from the wretched creature. "A draw, for now, Rascal." Something hit him squarely in the shoulder blade and he spun around, a scream caught in his throat. Shit. He'd backed into a tree; that was all.

He walked quickly out of the forest, looking over his shoulder every few feet to check that the animal wasn't following. When he reached the clearing, the grass sparse between outcroppings of rocks, he stopped to catch his breath.

He wasn't done with that 'coon. Now he'd have something to do in the godforsaken wilderness his father had dumped him in.

EIGHT

When Paige finally reached the parking lot where her green Honda was parked, her hands shook so bad it took three tries before she managed to press the unlock button on her key fob. Getting in, she sat still, taking deep breaths. This situation was affecting her more than she would have thought possible. It was making her slightly crazy, seeing things that weren't there.

Maybe a complete change of venue would help center her again. She could go see her mother, spend a couple of days with her. She sighed putting the key in the ignition. That wouldn't work. She loved her mother, but the woman had a tendency to cling. Paige knew seeing her mom would zap her strength rather than add to it. Besides, a visit out of the blue like that would make her mother worry even more than she already did.

No. This was on her. She'd have to deal with this on her own. She glanced up at the building where the law office was. Another day or two and she'd see things differently. She'd settle down and be able to get on with her career. She was about to back up out of the space when her cell phone dinged with a call.

Seeing Sheila's name come up, she clicked the button on the steering wheel. "Hi, Sheila."

"Paige. How are you doing today?" Her friend's voice was gentle with concern.

"Okay, I guess. A little hung-over if you want to know the truth. I probably shouldn't have had—"

"That too shall pass, my dear."

Paige spotted an opening to merge onto the street. "Another of your mum's sayings?"

"Nope. It doesn't matter though. It's true nonetheless. Would you like me to come over after work?"

"Thanks, but I'll be fine. Besides, you've got your hands full with the kids and John." Paige's smile faded picturing Sheila's family. She had everything going for her. A devoted husband with a great job and two nice kids, one in high school and the other not far behind. Someday she'd have that too.

"John can handle things for one night. Oh shit! I almost forgot Lesley's piano recital! Listen... Call me after nine if you want to talk or anything. And don't worry about work. Beth has rebooked all your appointments till Thursday."

Paige thought of the few clients that she'd scheduled for that day and Wednesday. None of them were terribly pressing. They were still at the letters-and-haggling stages, setting priorities to see if they could settle out of court. "Good. I should be back by Thursday."

"Well, take it easy, and don't put too much pressure on yourself. Go to a movie, or better yet, the spa. Get your nails done and have a massage."

Paige lifted her hand and glanced at her fingernails. They probably could use it, but it didn't seem right to pamper herself all things considered. "I'll think about it. Thanks for calling Sheila. Say hi to John and the kids."

"Sure. Take care, Paige." This was followed by a soft click disconnecting the call.

Traffic on the thoroughfare bypassing the outlying residential neighborhoods was busy considering it wasn't even rush hour. The gray Chevy ahead of her wasn't helping, barely traveling the speed limit. She glanced in the rearview mirror to check behind her and the passing lane. She jerked higher in the seat.

A child's face reflected in the mirror peered at her. Her head spun around, checking behind her, but of course, there was only the beige cushioned seat. No one there.

At the honk of a car to her left she turned the steering wheel, swerving the vehicle back to her own lane.

Her breath froze in her chest, and she gripped the wheel tighter. It had been Aubree's face there for a moment, staring at her! Oh my God. Was she *totally* losing it? She couldn't even do something as simple as driving without this happening?

With heart hammering fast, she tried to focus on the road. The traffic light just ahead was the one where she needed to turn. Thank God she was close to home. She probably shouldn't even be driving, seeing things that weren't there. How could this be happening?

Her forehead tightened. She'd learned something about this in school. The psychology classes with the professor going on about the subconscious mind, how powerful it is. That had to be it! The shock of the murder and how she had made that possible was playing out in her subconscious. Even to the extent that it was making her see this little girl everywhere.

She needed to deal with this, not try to get past it. Her subconscious was not going to let her sidestep any feelings of guilt. But she already felt guilty! For some reason that wasn't enough; she had to do more. But how? How to face her part in this, so she could put this behind her and resume her life?

At the last minute, she flipped her blinker on, signaling that she was going to turn into the church parking lot on the corner. It had been a long time since she'd darkened the door of a church, but maybe prayer would help. If nothing else the quiet and sense of peace in there would calm her. Mom had always sworn by prayer. She stopped the car and smirked. *Sworn* by prayer? Right. Her mouth twitched in a near smile at the oxymoron.

She put her cell phone on airplane mode as she got out of

the car. Leaves scuttled across the wide concrete steps of the white church and the breeze lifted blonde wisps of hair across her face. She tucked a lock behind her ear before she stepped up, holding the center rail firmly. The heavy oak door creaked as she pulled it open, and the smell of incense tickled her nostrils when she stepped inside.

At the end of the wooden rows of pews was the altar; the crucifix above it glowing in warm amber lighting. Aside from a few women seated in the front rows of the airy expanse, she was alone. Her sneakers squeaked on the marble floor as she entered the last row of seats. She sat quietly, head bowed, clasping her hands on her lap as she'd done as a little girl next to her mother.

Lord, if you're really there, I could use some help here. She didn't know when the tears started, but they rolled down her cheeks in a steady stream. Her shoulders racked with sobs—for the little girl, Aubree, and for her mother Noele.

I'm so very, very sorry. Please forgive me. For many more silent minutes, she sat there, alone. Gradually her tears slowed. She sniffed while pulling a tissue from her bag.

She sat quietly soaking in the silence, noticing rays of sunlight glinting through the stained glass. Every muscle in her body was warm and heavy. She took a deep breath, her gaze drifting to the crucifix and then to the gentle flames of the candles placed around it. She'd needed these moments of sanctuary.

She rose and walked slowly to the exit, pausing to put money in the charity box. There was peacefulness in her mind that hadn't been there since she'd first learned of the deaths. For that much, she was grateful.

She bathed in tranquility as she stepped out into the crisp autumn day. The leaves still clinging to the branches of maples and birches shimmered in red-and-gold waves from the sun's rays filtering through.

No, Sheila. A health spa couldn't rival the peace she felt now. This had been the right thing to do.

She walked with a steadier gait when she went to the car.

Before starting it, she reached in her purse for her cell phone to turn it back on. Jerking back, she saw that there had been a call but the sender was "Unknown." She hit a few numbers to retrieve the message.

When she heard the voice, she froze.

A young girl's voice: "Help me, Paige!"

NINE

Oh my god'. Paige stared at the phone with horror. Aubree. But that wasn't possible. The child was dead. She had to be mistaken.

Her fingers flew increasing the volume and then clicking the numbers to replay the message.

"Help me, Paige!"

There it was. Time stood still. The world outside her car no longer existed. She stared at the phone, her mind totally short-circuited. Catching glimpses of the girl at the periphery of her vision was one thing, but this message was another thing altogether.

It was proof that either she was the butt of an elaborate prank, or somehow this girl was contacting her from the afterlife.

The Afterlife.

The afterlife? But that couldn't be true. Growing up she'd listened to her share of ghost stories, seen her share of horror movies, but that was just made-up stuff to entertain you. It wasn't real, right?

Yet here on her phone was the voice of a little girl who was dead. The small voice had even called her by name!

Help her? It was far too late for that. But what did the child want her to do? What *could* she do?

This was crazy. Even accepting that this might be Aubree Smith, reaching out from the grave, there was nothing she could do.

She looked at the phone in her shaking hand. Her fingers once more tapped the buttons on the screen so that she could hear it again. Was she sure it was a little girl's voice? Could someone be playing a trick? Things like this; communications from beyond, couldn't really be happening.

She hoped.

A sigh drifted from her chest hearing the same message. There was no background noise in the message. The little girl's voice had been low and plaintive but clear nonetheless.

Paige set the phone down and started the car. From the article in the paper, she knew where Noele and Aubree had lived. The school where Aubree had just started grade one had also been mentioned. Maybe if she spoke to Aubree's teachers she'd get some kind of idea, some direction to go with this. Without it, she was coming up blank. She had to do *something* to make this stop.

A glance at the clock on the dash showed that it was just after three. Classes would be over for the day, but the teachers would still be there. She started the car and headed for the north end of the city where Noele had rented a house. The school was probably only a few blocks away from it.

Ten minutes later she pulled into the parking lot of a long brick building with a fenced playground area. She'd driven by this school a few times in the past. The crescent of letters above the door read *First Avenue Elementary*. This was it.

When she entered the building a smell, like caramels heating in a saucepan, hit her. A long hall lined with empty coat hooks extended before her. She followed the green tiles to the end where the main office was. Her mind scrambled as she walked, trying to come up with a logical reason why she'd be interested in talking to Aubree's teacher.

A middle-aged woman perched behind a computer monitor

looked up when Paige approached the front desk. Her smile was warm as she peered over her eyeglasses. "May I help you?"

"Yes. I'm Paige Wright. I understand Aubree Smith was a student here. I'd like to speak with her teachers, if I may. I was an attorney in the custody hearing." Paige crossed her fingers, holding her handbag close to her side.

Immediately the smile dropped from the secretary's face and was replaced with sadness. She rose to her feet and walked over to the counter. "It's so sad about that poor little girl and her mother. You were her attorney? I'll need to see some ID before I call Miss Wenford. There have been reporters who've tried to get more of an in-depth story...and well, you know."

Paige nodded. "I understand." She rummaged in her purse and pulled out a business card from the firm as well as her Bar Association card. But before she could hand them over, another young woman walked into the office.

"What's up, Meaghan?"

Paige looked over at the woman. Jet-black hair framed an oval face while her dark eyes flashed between the secretary and Paige.

The secretary cleared her throat and answered, "This woman is a lawyer who is interested in seeing you about Aubree. But, I've asked her for—"

"You know Mrs. Smith, or rather, knew Mrs. Smith and her daughter?"

Paige handed over her credentials to the new woman. She glanced at it and then looked at Paige, waiting for a reply.

Her words were rushed and she hoped convincing. "Mrs. Smith, yes; of course I knew her. But Aubree, I'm afraid I never met her. I'm curious in light of what happened." She felt her cheeks grow warm and decided that she'd better try for honesty. "Actually, I've been thinking a lot about Aubree. I feel that I need to know more about her. I know it sounds odd, but I can't get her out of my mind." That much was the truth.

The young woman placed her hand on Paige's shoulder. "I'm Nellie Wenford. Aubree was my student. Come with me to my classroom and we'll talk."

"But Nellie, we really—"

Nellie cut the secretary off. "It's okay Meaghan. If the principal has any problem with this, I'll take responsibility." She walked out of the office and slowed for Paige to fall into step next to her. "Although it was a shock reading about Aubree's and her mother's deaths, I knew things weren't right at her home. Aubree was a sweet kid, eager to learn and do things when she was here. She made friends easily. But at the end of each day, a pall came over her."

Paige looked over at the teacher. "A pall? That's pretty somber."

Nellie smiled and looked down at the floor. "Yeah, maybe. That sounds weird I know, but there was definitely a sadness that she couldn't hide, or in retrospect, it was probably fear. Don't get me wrong. She adored her mother. You could see they were close when she'd come in to pick Aubree up. It didn't happen that often as she worked shifts, and most days Aubree took the school bus home. But they'd both light up like candles when they saw each other on the days she could come."

Paige followed the teacher into a room where small chairs and tables were set in a semicircle. Shelves of books were set against one wall while a play area with a rug littered with sets of colorful cushioned blocks sat at the back. The teacher led the way to a desk which was bare of objects, unlike others where pictures and pencil crayons scattered over the surfaces. She didn't need the teacher to tell her that it was the desk where Aubree had sat.

"You knew that things weren't right at home for Aubree."

The teacher's head dipped to the side for a moment. "Well, there was a restraining order on the father. We were under strict orders. Only Mrs. Smith was authorized to pick Aubree up from school. That and Aubree's attitude regarding going home told me plenty. I wish you'd called me as a witness during that custody hearing. It might have turned out differently. Why didn't you?"

Paige's mouth dried up, and she had to turn from the

young woman's gaze. Finally, she answered, "I'm sorry you didn't testify. But, Miss Wenford—"

"Nellie, please. My students call me Miss Wenford."

Oh God. This was going to be even harder. "Nellie. I'm ashamed to admit this, but I represented the father."

"What?" The teacher's chin dropped as she stepped backward. In a split second, the expression on her face changed. There was a coldness in her eyes that belied her former warmth. "What the hell are you doing here? What do you want, Ms. Wright?"

Paige's hand rose, and her eyes closed for a moment. "Please. You have no idea how bad I feel about that."

"Bad? I'm supposed to feel sorry for the person who enabled this to happen? You defended that monster's rights and now Aubree's dead!" Her arm rose, pointing at the door of the classroom. "Get out of here, right now!"

"I'm sorry!" Again tears welled in Paige's eyes. "You have no idea how sorry I am! I'd do anything to change what happened, but I can't." She slumped lower, catching her hand on Aubree's desk.

"Is that why you're here? This is some kind of sick penance? Well if you're looking for sympathy, it's between shit and syphilis in the dictionary!" The teacher turned and strode over to her desk, putting it as a barrier between them.

"I'm not looking for sympathy. I'm looking for answers! I need to know about Aubree. What was she like? What does she want?" Even to her own ears, it sounded crazy. And this teacher wasn't about to cut her any slack.

"What does she *want*?" The young woman's face twisted into a knot as she rounded the desk to glare at Paige. "She sure as hell didn't want to be choked to death by her own father! You've got some nerve—"

"Please! I'm seeing Aubree everywhere!" When the woman's eyes narrowed she scooped her phone from her purse. She pressed the keys to retrieve her voice mail and in a rush of words, "Listen! Listen to this, and tell me if you recognize her voice."

The teacher's gaze flitted between the cell phone and Paige's eyes. She held the phone higher waiting for the child's voice to sound. But there was only dead air.

Frantically she hit the numbers again, mumbling, "Hang on. I just listened to this. Where is—"

"You're nuts." The teacher's hands rose before her chest as she backed away. "I have no idea what you're up to but I've heard enough. You'll have to leave." She lifted her arm and pointed to the classroom door. "Right now before I call the police!"

TEN

Paige felt her cheeks grow warm as she left the classroom. She didn't blame the teacher. The woman had obviously cared for the little girl. Why would she show a modicum of empathy for the person representing the guy who'd murdered Aubree?

Her eyes narrowed. Why hadn't that message on the phone played? Three times in the car it had gone off without a hitch. True, she'd been upset, but could she have accidentally erased it? Damn it. The teacher would have been able to confirm that it was Aubree's voice if the message had played.

When she reached her car, she scanned the phone for any indication that there'd been a message and that she'd erased it. But nothing came up—not even call history. She stared ahead, seeing nothing while her mind replayed everything from leaving the church to deciding to visit the school. She'd heard it three times! But now there was no record of ever getting a call.

This was crazy. She gave her head a shake and started the car. It was time to go home and try to put this behind her. Either that or make an appointment to see a shrink. Guilt and remorse were understandable, but at this level; making her see the little girl...hell, even hearing a message...it was way over the top.

Still...setting this aside was easier said than done.

When she arrived home, she clicked on the computer for any news that maybe Cory Smith had been found. But there were no new headlines. Nothing. How hard could it be to find the guy when his picture was plastered on every news site in the country? Surely someone had seen him.

She hadn't eaten since having a piece of toast earlier, but the thought of lunch made her stomach roll.

She wandered into her bedroom and picked up the book she'd been reading. It was a mystery novel. It might succeed in taking her mind off the murder of that little girl. After settling on her bed, she read and then reread a few pages, but the words weren't registering.

The scene in the courtroom, Noele's testimony played in her head. Why hadn't she seen the sincerity, heard the abject pleading in her voice? Her dark eyes had filled with tears describing a scene where Cory had grabbed Aubree's arm, his other hand raised to strike the young preschooler. When the mother had intervened, he had turned on her. She claimed that he'd beaten her yet she hadn't called for help. A couple of days had even passed before she went to the police.

If only she'd heard the cry for help instead of blindly pointing out the inconsistencies in Noele's account.

Maybe if she hadn't been so willing to fight for a father's rights to raise his daughter, she would have.

A father's rights.

Her jaw tightened. Her own mother had denied those same damn rights to *her* father. If her mother had allowed the man, who was Paige's father, to even *meet* his daughter, maybe she wouldn't have defended Cory's case so hard. It wasn't like Paige had never asked about him. But her mother had always refused to let her know *anything* about him.

Her lips became a firm line. It was the only thing her mother refused when it came to Paige. Even though Mom never made that much money, she made sure that Paige never wanted for anything—the latest fashion or gadget that all her other friends owned. But knowing who her father was never made that list. It was the one thing she'd never forgive her mother for.

She set the book aside and slid lower on the bed. That line of thinking was getting her nowhere fast. And considering the horrible night's sleep she'd had, a nap might make her feel better. Certainly, second-guessing the past wasn't helping. She tugged the comforter over herself, even tucking it over her head. In less than a minute she was out like a light.

***

Paige awoke with a start, her heart beating fast. She'd had that dream again! But this time the backyard had seemed even more real; there were details now that hadn't been there before. There'd been a bee flitting in a mound of orange chrysanthemums next to an aged wooden fence. And the little girl—who had to be Aubree—was wearing a red plaid jacket above stonewashed jeans. The same damn coat the child in the park had been wearing! She could feel the girl's panic, staring at the back door of the house. Even the details of the home, a mustard-colored bungalow with burgundy shutters stuck out in Paige's mind.

A glance at the clock on her bedside table showed that it was only a half past four. The light coming in her bedroom window was dull reflecting the sun lower in the sky. It was still early enough. She threw the comforter off and sat up, only then aware of coming to a decision.

She had to visit the girl's house. There was no way her mind was playing tricks on her earlier that day. She had seen the child! Three times in fact, and she'd heard the girl ask for help, specifically saying her name. She might regret this decision later on, and even question her own sanity for doing it, but for now, it was the right thing to do.

She grabbed her jacket from the chair where she'd left it. After verifying the address of the house on Victoria Avenue, from the news article, she popped her phone into her bag. The surge of adrenaline that she'd woken with was still pumping fast, but her sense of calm told her she was correct in doing this.

She parked the car on the quiet residential street and looked at the house. She hadn't needed the house number to find it. Ribbons of yellow police tape draped along the front step blocking the entrance to the crime scene. But it was the house itself that took her breath away. It was that same mustard yellow with burgundy shutters from her dream. Any doubt that she had been right in going there evaporated in that moment.

There was no way she was going to cross that police tape, which wasn't really a problem anyway. It was the backyard that had been the focus of the dream; that's where she saw the child playing, and that's where she was headed.

She looked down the alley between the house and the one next to it, and got out of the car. Just a peek at the yard. A quick glance up and down the street showed that all was quiet. No neighbors out or even anyone out walking their dog. The houses were uniform wartime small bungalows, popular for young families and those on fixed incomes.

She walked quickly down the strip of grass, brushing by a garden hose looped on a hanger and low-lying shrubs lining the concrete foundation. A four-foot wooden fence with a gate was just ahead at the corner of the house. And, thank God, no yellow tape. Peeking in, she gasped seeing the old tree with the swing and the sandbox off to the side. Even the orange flowers, tucked in next to the worn wooden fence, made her heart skip a beat.

It was exactly like her dream!

She pressed the latch and pushed the gate wide. Although the fence was high and the possibility of being seen by the neighbors was remote, Paige crouched a little as she stepped into the yard, closing the gate softly behind her. She stayed close to the fence, watching the swing sway slightly in the breeze. It wasn't hard to imagine the little girl on the tire swing, swooping higher and higher in the air. She swallowed hard as her fingers touched the rough rope.

The sandbox pulled at her gaze where a red plastic shovel poked up from a small mound. She approached as slowly as a pallbearer. At the edge of the play space, gazing down at the innocent toy, she felt tears sting the back of her eyes.

The sharp bang behind her made her almost jump out of her skin. Spinning around she saw it was only the screen door that had blown wide, thudding against the frame when the spring yanked it closed.

Turning back to the sandbox she bent down and scooped up a handful of sand, letting it drift through her fingers—the same sand that Aubree had played in. She was about to reach for the plastic shovel when a half-buried object caught her attention. A circle of pink beads lay half covered by the light sand. She picked it up. It was a child's bracelet, colorful beads encircling a silver medallion.

The familiar MedicAlert logo, a serpent coiled around a staff inscribed with *Diabetes-Type One* glinted back at her. The bracelet was barely big enough to enclose her fingers, even though the pearly pink beads were threaded by elastic. She slipped it into her palm, closing her hand around it.

Aubree.

This MedicAlert bracelet had been hers. A picture of the child flashed in her mind, the little girl intent on creating a castle in the sand, never noticing that the bracelet had caught on the handle of the shovel. The next scene in her mind was Aubree slowly backing away, staring at the back door. Paige could feel the terror in the little girl's body, watching her father approach.

Tears ran down Paige's cheeks as she hunched next to the sandbox. Everything in her dream was exactly as what she saw here. The little girl had somehow reached out to her for help, first appearing in her bathroom last night, and then in the park and her car. She'd even used the time where Paige had been in the church seeking solace to leave a more concrete message, although there was no trace of it now.

The peace that seeped into Paige's body was further confirmation that she'd been meant to come here, to find this.

She sniffed and took a deep breath looking at the bracelet. "What now? I've found this, but what does it mean?"

But this time, only the silence in the yard answered.

ELEVEN

As Paige prepared dinner, her gaze was continually drawn to the bracelet on the kitchen table beside her laptop. Should she try to contact any living relatives of the child to give it to them? Surely a grandparent would want it as a keepsake. But they'd also wonder how she got it.

The knife she gripped slipped from the cucumber and nicked her finger. For a moment she stared at the blood seeping from the cut before giving her head a shake and turning on the kitchen faucet. It stung really bad—like a kind of penance. She kept her finger under the faucet gritting her teeth at the pain. When it subsided she swathed the wound in a paper towel to staunch the bleeding.

She tossed the vegetables into the salad bowl and took it over to the kitchen table. A few clicks on the laptop to her favorite news site showed the same things she'd already heard. No update that they'd located the father. Cory was still at large.

Taking a bite, she again gazed at the bracelet. There was no doubt that she'd been directed to finding it. First the dream last night and then again that afternoon. She'd caught glimpses of the young girl, and heard her plea for help.

Toying with the small bracelet, her fingers rolled the beads softly. She would keep the bracelet. For some reason Aubree wanted her to find it.

She sighed reading the silver inscription. *Diabetes-Type One.* She'd gone to elementary school with a kid who had that. He'd been able to manage it with pills, but still, there were days when he'd had to sit in the classroom while the rest of the kids went outside for the afternoon recess. Had Aubree been tired too? But the teacher hadn't mentioned anything about that.

She finished eating and slipped the bracelet into her pocket. After she tidied up the counter, she was about to stack her cutlery and bowl in the dishwasher when she paused. A comforting billow, like the warmth of a fireplace on a winter's night, rolled over her.

She couldn't say she was happy. Two people were dead, and she couldn't deny her part in their deaths, but she wasn't overwrought like she had been.

It was more than that. It wasn't just the absence of agitation, but she felt a sense of peace. She never thought she'd feel that way again. It was even greater than what she'd felt leaving the church.

Her hand slid over the small bulge in her pocket where the bracelet was nestled. It was because of that bracelet.

Aubree had directed her to it.

Which was a crazy thought. The child's dead, so how…? Paige took a deep breath and blew it out as she shook her head. It doesn't matter. As crazy as it seemed, she knew it was true.

But now that she had the bracelet, what was next?

She continued with the kitchen cleanup and was about to leave to go into the living room when her cell phone rang. It was probably Sheila checking in on her. She grabbed it from her handbag and glanced at the screen.

Karen?

Her heart did a somersault while she gaped at the phone. There had to be something wrong at home for Karen to call.

"Hello? Karen?"

"Hi, Paige. I'm afraid I have some bad news. Your

mother...she had a stroke. She's—"

"Is she all right? Is she alive?" Paige's eyes were wide staring at the floor, seeing nothing. Oh my God.

"Yes. She's in the hospital. She's in intensive care and they're doing tests. They won't know the extent of the damage for twenty-four hours. The doctors said it was lucky I found her and got her in so quickly." Her voice broke. "We always watch *The Price Is Right* together! That's how I found her."

Paige's eyes teared up. The two women were next door neighbors and best friends, like something out of a TV show. "She's lucky to have you, Karen."

"You're coming here, right?"

"Of course. I'll leave right away. Are you at home or at the hospital?"

"I'm at the hospital. I'll stay until you get here."

"Karen, it's a three hour drive." Maybe two and a half if she punched it, but still.

"Don't be silly. Someone has to be here. Maybe they'll know something sooner than they expect." The poor woman sounded worn out. This was hitting her hard too.

"I'll see you soon as I can." With that, Paige clicked the phone off and put it back in her bag. She grabbed her coat and was about to head out when she stopped. She'd probably be gone for a few days. Rushing to her bedroom she grabbed her suitcase from the closet and threw some clothes in it. Next the laptop.

Oh my God. Tears threatened to spill, but she took a deep breath heading out the door. Karen had said her mother was okay, that she'd gotten medical help in good time. She had to think positive thoughts. Furthermore, how could she drive if she was bawling her eyes out?

She got in her car and headed for the highway. Three hours away. Her gut sank remembering how she'd dismissed the earlier thought of visiting her mother. There'd been too many times when she had been too busy, too caught up in her own life to make that trip to see her mother. And now this? This is what it took to get her home?

Home. Yeah. The small town was still home even after being away for almost ten years. She could still see her mother making dinner, listening to Paige tell her about school that day. And then later, the two of them snuggled on the sofa watching TV, eating popcorn.

Sinking lower still in the seat as she merged onto the highway, a more recent picture of her mother flooded her mind. Mom was obese. It was small wonder that she'd had a stroke. The woman ate too many fatty foods, too many bags of potato chips watching the television alone at night. She'd tried to get her mother into Weight Watchers. She'd even paid for a year's membership at the health club, but she'd never gone.

Things would be different after this. She'd visit more often, and make sure her mother lived a healthier lifestyle.

If this stroke didn't kill her first.

TWELVE

It was a little after eleven PM when Paige rushed through the doors of the hospital. The only time she'd ever been in there was when she visited her friend Melanie who'd had her tonsils out. But she could remember the smell—antiseptic mixed with a pine scent from the cleaning solutions. She brushed by the reception where a security guard sat reading something on his cell phone.

Shit. The cell phone reminded her. She'd have to call Sheila and let her know she'd be away the rest of the week. She hadn't answered the three calls from her friend while she was driving. Hearing her voice was bound to unleash tears telling Sheila about her mother.

The waiting room was around the corner just up ahead. Sure enough, Karen was there perched on the edge of a sofa.

She looked up when the door opened, and Paige walked in. "Oh God, Paige; I'm so glad you're here."

Paige took a seat next to the middle-aged woman and put her hand on her shoulder. "Any word? Do you think they'll let me see her?"

Karen shook her head slowly. "Nothing yet. But maybe that's a good—"

"Hang on." Paige stood up and headed for the nurses' station down the corridor. At the low counter she stopped, and ignoring the fact that the nurse was writing some file notes, she interrupted, "Excuse me, but I'm here about Mrs. Wright? She's my mother. I'd like to see her."

The nurse looked up at her, her face impassive. She turned her head slowly to look at the clock and back to Paige before she shook her head. "It's eleven o'clock, ma'am. Visiting hours are over. You'll have to come back—"

"No! I need to see her now!" Paige caught herself. She was right on the edge of losing it after the day she'd had. She took a deep breath. "Look, she had a stroke, and I've just driven three hours to be with her."

The nurse's mouth set in a thin line.

Before she could say anything else, Paige kept her voice gentle. "Hey...what if it was you standing here asking? What if it were *your* mom?"

The nurse sighed as she stood. But a small smile curved her lips now. "Okay." Her eyes flashed. "But you have to be *quiet*, understand?"

Paige held her hands up. "Sure! Sure!"

"But only for five minutes. You really need to stay quiet though. Other patients are trying to sleep." With a sideways nod of her head, the nurse then led the way down the hall.

Paige wasn't quite ready to let out a sigh of relief. That would depend on the condition she found her mother in.

It was a large room with four beds. Patients lay sleeping while plastic tubes and wires connected them to monitoring equipment. Her mother was in the first bed to the right. She brushed past the nurse and hurried to her mother's side, placing her hand gently over her mother's.

The tears that she'd fought on the drive there now spilled down her cheeks. Her mother looked helpless and so...old. When did that happen? It had been a couple months since she'd visited with her mother. And now, the poor woman was barely hanging on, not even aware she was there.

"Mom? I'm here." Her throat tightened, and she was

unable to get words out louder than a whisper. She wanted to tell her mother that she'd be better soon, but how could she say that when the only sign that she was alive was the rise and fall of her chest? And even that was faint, aided by an oxygen tube snaking across her plump cheeks to rest under her nose.

Her mother's eyelids fluttered and then creaked open a slit, becoming wider when it registered that Paige was there.

"It's okay, Mom. Don't try to speak. I'm here now." She smiled seeing her mother's lips part and the slight nod of her head. Her gaze dropped, and she squeezed her mother's hand slightly to reassure her. The fact that she'd recognized Paige was a good sign, right? Maybe the damage wasn't that bad?

At the touch on her arm, Paige looked over at the nurse. The nurse's lips were tight before she whispered, "She needs to rest now."

After one long last look at her mother, Paige stepped away from the bed following the other woman from the room. The nurse turned when they were in the hallway. "You can come back tomorrow at ten to see her again."

But Paige had other plans. "I'm staying in the waiting room tonight. I want to know that she's okay. She will be, right?"

Glancing over her shoulder and back to Paige the nurse took a deep breath. "She didn't have a massive stroke, but"—she fluttered her hands up— "it was a stroke."

Paige's heart sank. "What do you mean?"

"I mean it's serious." Seeing the look on Paige's face, she reached out and held her forearm. "It could have been worse, but it's still serious, okay?" She paused for a second. "What's your name?"

"Paige." She tilted her head. "Just tell me. I can handle bad news."

"Okay. Look, your mother is receiving tissue plasminogen. That's good meds working to dissolve clots and improve blood flow to the part of her brain that was affected."

The shock must have shown on Paige's face because the nurse added. "We'll have a better idea tomorrow." She tilted her head. "You're planning on staying here all night?"

"Yeah."

"Okay. I'll see about getting you a blanket." With that, the nurse left her. Paige looked at the room where her mother was hooked up to tubes and gadgets. She said a silent prayer as she waited for the nurse to return. "Please, God, let her be okay."

She took the white cotton blanket from the nurse and then returned to the waiting room where Karen still sat. She took a seat next to the middle-aged woman once more. "They think it might have been a blood clot that did this."

"Your mother's a fighter, Paige." Karen squeezed Paige's hand, staring deeply into Paige's eyes. "It will be okay."

Paige nodded absently. What the hell else could the woman say? She didn't know that things would work out. None of them did. "I'll stay here tonight, Karen. You've done enough. Go home and get some sleep. I'll call you if anything changes."

Karen sighed and then looked down at her lap for a moment. "Okay. But I can be back here in twenty minutes if you need me. I'll come again in the morning." She stood up and slipped the strap of her purse over her shoulder. "Try to get some sleep, Paige. This has been rough for you as well."

"Yeah." She looked down. Karen didn't know the half of it.

Karen touched her shoulder. "Your mother said she was going to call you before bed tonight, but..." Her eyes glistened, and she waved at their surroundings.

Paige nodded silently as Karen pecked her on the cheek. She watched as the woman turned to leave. She seemed to have aged ten years. The strain showed in her slow steps across the room. Karen was also Paige's godmother. She'd spent a lot of time in Karen's house as a child.

Paige spread the blanket over her shoulders and tucked her feet up on the sofa. If her mother survived this she'd make up for all the times she had been too busy to visit. Please, God, let that happen. She settled in for a long night.

THIRTEEN

When her cell phone buzzed Paige's eyes popped open. She sat up. When she saw the name on the phone, her eyes shut for a moment. Of course, it was Sheila. Damn it. She'd forgot to return Sheila's calls.

"Sheila? I'm sorry I didn't call you last night."

"Paige. Are you all right? I was so worried."

"Yes...but my mom. Oh my God, Sheila. She had a stroke. I'm at the hospital now, and I spent the night." She flipped the blanket off her shoulders and sat forward.

"What? Is she okay?" Sheila's words came out in a rush.

"I don't know. The doctors said they will have a better idea of the damage today. I won't be at work tomorrow. Actually, I'm not sure if I'll even be in next week. I've got vacation time that—"

"Don't worry about it, Paige. You've got to see to your mother first. Bradley will understand, and if he doesn't… Well, I'm also a partner there, so I've got some say in that."

"Thanks, Sheila. I'll call you later after I've talked to the doctors. They've got her on blood thinners and oxygen, so they might have helped overnight." Paige prayed that her mother would be awake and that the damage would be minimal.

"Okay, then. Just let me know if there's anything I can do."

"Thanks. I will. I'll call you later." Paige clicked the phone off and rose to her feet. There had to be a coffee shop or vending machine around somewhere. It was only a little before eight. Too soon to go in to see her mother.

A couple of nurses in colorful uniforms opened the door and were heading across the room about to enter the unit where her mother lay. It looked like a shift change. Much as she wanted a coffee, she decided to stay put in the hopes that the nurse who'd been there last night would come out.

She didn't have that long to wait before the nurse from the night before appeared, pushing a stray lock of brown hair behind her ear as she entered the waiting room. Paige jerked to her feet, "Excuse me. My mother, Cheryl Wright—how is she?"

The nurse paused. "She had a good night. Her blood pressure is lower now, which is a good thing. The neurologist will be in this afternoon to examine her." The nurse's eyes were red-rimmed from her twelve-hour shift but even so, there was kindness in her expression. "I'm afraid that's all I can tell you for now."

Paige let out a long sigh of relief, only then aware that she'd been holding her breath. "Thanks." As the nurse was about to leave, she quickly asked, "Is there somewhere I can get a coffee?"

"Yes. If you go to the lower level there's a cafeteria where you can get coffee and something to eat."

***

It was quarter to ten when Karen showed up at the hospital again. She hurried across the waiting room carrying takeout coffee and a small paper sack. "Any news? How is she?"

Paige took the coffee and smiled up at her. "The nurse from last night said she's doing better. At least her blood pressure is down."

Karen looked up at the ceiling. "Thank God." She settled in

next to Paige and opened the sack of pastries. "Here. These are from O'Brien's. Remember how good their cranberry biscuits are? Have one."

Paige took the still warm pastry from the bag and bit into it. She'd finish this and then it would be time to get in to see her mother. "She smiled and nodded her head, silently thanking Karen for this kindness. "Delicious."

Karen popped the top from her coffee and took a sip. "I let the store know about Cheryl. Jenny was pretty upset to hear about it. She asked if there was anything she could do and to let her know when she could come in to see your mom."

"That's nice of her." Paige could picture Jenny and the small grocery store. Her mother had worked there for as long as Paige could remember. Jenny was more like a friend than a boss to her mother.

The door to the waiting room opened, and a doctor in his mid-thirties stepped through. "Miss Wright?" His gaze fell on Paige's face, and he stepped over, extending his hand.

She rose and shook his hand. "Yes. I'm Paige Wright. My mother—"

"She's doing fine. Actually, she's awake. The nurse on duty told me that you'd spent the night, so I thought you'd be anxious to see her. I'm Dr. Morris." He smiled and then pushed the bridge of his eyeglasses higher on his face.

"Did she say anything? Oh God, I was so worried." She fell into step beside him, but before she went through the door, she turned to Karen. "I'll be right back. I'll let you know how she's doing."

The doctor looked over at her and his smile fell. "Your mother...she tried to talk. That's a good sign. At least her face muscles are working. Based on the tests we completed when she arrived, it was a blood clot affecting blood supply to the Broca area. The neurologist will speak to you about that later once he examines her. But for now, your mother probably will have trouble speaking."

Paige's heart stopped. "She can't talk?"

"No, but it's not that bad. She'll just be having a hard time finding the right words. She'll"—he made grasping gestures in the air—"she'll have trouble with processing her thoughts to spoken words. Her ability to speak is fine, it's the underpinning wiring that's off."

"Is that permanent?"

"Not usually. In most cases fluency in language returns." He paused at the door to her mother's room and gestured for her to enter.

Paige gaped at him for a few moments before entering the room. Trouble speaking? How would her mother manage? She stepped inside and rushed to the bedside. Her color seemed better with a faint hint of pink in her cheeks, while her blue eyes crinkled seeing her daughter. "Mom! How are you doing?" Remembering what the doctor had said about her mother's ability to talk, she quickly added, "They say you had a good night. That your blood pressure is better."

The doctor took a spot on the other side of the bed. "Mrs. Wright, I'm Dr. Morris. You experienced a cerebrovascular accident, or as is commonly referred to as a stroke, yesterday afternoon. You were lucky that your neighbor found you and called for help so quickly. Time is really critical with incidents like this."

Her mother's mouth opened and closed a few times before the doctor placed his hand on her shoulder. "The left side of the brain experienced loss of blood flow, so your speech may be difficult right now. The neurologist, Dr. Bennet will be in later today. In the meantime, we'll run more tests and see how things are looking after your night on blood thinner."

Paige could see the panic settle in her mother's eyes. She leaned in closer and spoke softly, "Remember those medical shows you like so much? How you're always amazed at what modern medicine can do? You'll be fine, Mom, and I'm not leaving your side until you are."

Paige looked over at the doctor hoping he'd chime in, reassuring her mother and herself that what she'd said was true. But his expression was unreadable.

She turned back to her mother, anxious to calm her fears.

"Karen's outside. She called Jenny. Boy oh boy, the things you'll do to get a few days off, Mom." Paige grinned to let her know she was teasing. "Seriously, she said not to worry about work, but to just get better."

The doctor cleared his throat. "I'll check in later to see how you're doing." He stepped back and then reached to tug the curtain from where it bunched at the wall, giving them privacy from the other patients.

Paige sat with her mother. It was only when Cheryl's eyes grew heavy and closed that she got up to stretch her legs. Even if her mother couldn't speak, it was good to see her awake and that she was being cared for.

Paige left the room and went out to the waiting area where Karen was perched, her fingers quickly working the knitting needles while a red square of some project rested on her lap. She looked up when Paige walked over. "How is she?"

Paige sighed. "She just fell asleep."

Karen slid the knitting project into a tapestry bag and stood up. "Why don't you go home. I mean to Cheryl's place, not Albany. Have a shower and change your clothes. It'll make you feel better, and by the time you return here, she might be awake again. It'll only take you an hour. The neurologist won't be in until the afternoon."

Paige nodded. "I think I will." She looked at Karen. "Call me if they come out with any news though. I'll be as quick as I can. Do you want me to pick up some lunch for you?"

Karen patted her oversized bag. "I brought sandwiches for both of us. But if you'd rather have something—"

"No. That sounds great. I'll take you up on that when I get back." She turned and called over her shoulder, "See you soon."

***

Paige drove to her mother's home and parked the car in the short driveway. She sat quietly for a few moments looking at the home she'd grown up in as if seeing it for the first time. When had the paint grown so shabby, flaking off near the windows at the front of the house? And the house was so tiny. The walkway leading up to the front step was narrow, the low shrubs bordering it in need of a good pruning.

She pulled her keys from the ignition and thumbed through until she came to the worn silver key to the front door. She grabbed her overnight bag from the back seat and then walked up the cracked cement sidewalk. When she opened the door the familiar fragrance of pumpkin spice welcomed her. At this time of year, her mother always filled the house with candles scented with the smell of autumn.

After slipping her sneakers off, she stepped into the short hallway separating the kitchen from the living room. The place was the same except that the clutter had grown even more. A stack of magazines and newspapers threatened to slip from the small table in the hallway while the coatrack above was layered with coats and scarves each clinging precariously to the set of brass coat hooks.

She edged by a plant stand and entered the bedroom where she'd spent the first eighteen years of her life. Setting the suitcase on the pink patchwork quilt topping the narrow bed, she looked around the room. A series of school pictures from grade one to college graduation were edged into the frame of the mirror above a chest of drawers. Even the poster of Nickleback was still on the wall next to the tiny closet. Her mother hadn't changed anything in the room, keeping it like a shrine. It was probably the only room in the house that wasn't jammed with stuff.

Giving her head a shake, she pulled the bag of toiletries from the suitcase. She was here to be with her mother, and she'd better get a move on if she was going to be able to speak to that neurologist.

As she was peeling her jeans off to step into the shower her fingers paused at the small lump in her pocket.

Aubree's MedicAlert bracelet.

She set it on the vanity and stepped out of her jeans. There wasn't anything she could do about the bracelet now. She had her mother to worry about. But trying to convince her gut of that was easier said than done. She tried to focus on completing her shower to get back to the hospital.

After rinsing the shampoo from her hair, she turned the spray off. When she pulled the shower curtain back, a glance at the vanity gave her a start.

The bracelet was gone.

With narrow eyes she peered at the floor to see if perhaps it had fallen. But a quick scan of her jeans and shirt resting on the green tile showed only her clothes. She grabbed a clean towel from the rack next to the tub and tucked it around herself before stepping out.

For sure, she'd felt the bracelet in her pocket and had removed it, setting it on the vanity. She was positive she'd done that! Even though it had been a rough night's sleep on the hard hospital sofa, her brain was still functioning... Wasn't it?

Rummaging through the clothes on the floor, she felt the small beads and the silver band in the jeans. Her breath hitched in her chest as her hand slipped into the pocket, and she pulled out the bracelet.

This wasn't possible. She'd set the thing on the counter, yet there it was back in her pocket. For a few moments she could only stare at it, her heart fluttering fast.

Her gaze flitted across the room. Had someone entered the house? She hadn't locked the front door when she'd come in, but no one here ever did, not during the day at least. For Pete's sake it was a small town, not Albany.

She took a deep breath and called out, "Hello?" But the quiet of the house was the only answer.

Giving her head another shake, she whispered, "Of course there's no one here. And even if a neighbor or Jenny popped in to see about Mom, they sure as hell wouldn't come into the bathroom hearing me in the shower."

Still, she tucked the towel tighter and clicked the lock on the bathroom door. That was definitely weird, finding the bracelet back in her pocket. But everything about the little girl and her bracelet was odd.

She toweled off quickly and then got dressed again. The jeans weren't dirty, just slept in, and she hadn't brought that many clothes aside from fresh undies. A quick comb through of her hair, tying it into a wet ponytail, and she was just about done. She brushed her teeth and put on a dab of lipstick to add some color to her tired face. All the while she pushed thoughts of the bracelet to the far recesses of her brain, focusing on being done with this and on her way back to see her mother.

Nevertheless, before she left the house, she did a quick check on each room, opening closet doors to make sure there was no one there. Part of her wished that she'd find a neighbor. It would be better than being alone and knowing that the bracelet had moved by itself.

As she drove she dipped her head to each shoulder, stretching her neck muscles. She was wound up wire tight from all this. First the murder, catching glimpses of the little girl and now her mother's illness. Who wouldn't be tense after all that?

But the bracelet...

She couldn't shake the feeling that Aubree was still reaching out to her.

FOURTEEN

When Paige entered the room where she'd visited with her mother that morning the bed was empty. Her heart kicked into overdrive as she hurried to the nurses' station. "My mother! Where's my mother, Cheryl Wright?"

The same doctor she'd talked to earlier stepped over to the counter, leaving the side of the middle-aged nurse he'd been speaking with. He held his hands up. "Your mother's fine. She's in radiology for tests. Dr. Bennett is scheduled to see her in a couple of hours."

Paige's chest emptied with relief. Of course. He'd said something about doing more tests earlier.

Dr. Morris rounded the counter and stood before her. "They're doing a CAT scan to determine the extent of the damage. From her blood work it was clear that it was a clot, not a hemorrhage, in the brain. That's actually good news."

Even though the doctor's expression and tone was meant to be reassuring Paige was still shook up from seeing her mother's empty bed.

"Look, I'll let you know as soon as she's back from radiology. You can see her then. I'm pretty sure Bennett will want you there when he talks to her." He had stepped away from the desk, leading her back down the hall to the waiting room.

She nodded. "Thanks, Dr. Morris." Leaving him behind, she walked slowly to the waiting room to join Karen again.

"That was quick. How is she?" Karen set her knitting aside and patted the place next to her on the sofa.

"I didn't see her. They're doing more tests." She slumped into the spot beside her godmother and sighed. "The doctor said he'll let me know when she's back." She looked into Karen's gray eyes, "I feel awful. I never visited her as often as I should have. Maybe I could have seen this coming...done something to prevent it."

Karen patted her knee, leaning closer. "You couldn't have known. I popped over every day when she'd come home from work, and I never saw this coming, Paige. You can't blame yourself." She looked away and her jaw tightened. "There are things that happen which you can't control. Really *bad things*."

A picture of Karen's deceased husband flitted through Paige's mind. He'd died behind the wheel of his transport over fifteen years ago. But somehow she had the feeling that Karen wasn't thinking of Walter right then.

The murder in Albany jumped to the forefront of Paige's brain. Really bad things do happen, all right. "You heard about that murder in Albany?"

Karen nodded, closing her eyes for a couple beats. "Yes. I was just thinking about that. It's such a shame. That poor little girl and her mother." Shaking her head sadly, she added, "How could someone do that?"

Paige had always been close to Karen. Her voice faltered when she spoke. "Did you know that I defended the husband, Cory Smith, in a child custody battle?" Paige felt the tears stinging behind her eyes but she pressed on. "I enabled that man to have access to them. The police still haven't found him."

Karen's eyes became wide staring at her. "Oh my God."

Paige slumped lower in her seat. "It's my fault."

Karen swallowed hard and leaned closer. "It's *not* your fault. You couldn't have known what he'd do. Some people are just born bad. It's in their genes."

Paige pictured Cory and for the hundredth time asked herself how she'd missed it. Had he been born bad as Karen seemed to think? What else could account for people like Paul Bernardo and Ted Bundy? Was it in their genes or could their upbringing account for some of it?

"I wish I'd never laid eyes on Cory Smith. I feel tangled up in his treachery." Tears that she'd bottled up gave way when Karen pulled her close.

Karen stroked Paige's hair and then eased back. "You couldn't have known what would happen. The world is full of tragedy, things that none of us can control. You've got to let this go, Paige. It'll eat you up until you do."

Paige plucked a tissue from the box on the coffee table and wiped her eyes. Karen was probably right about stepping back from the nightmare murder. But that wasn't likely to happen.

When she eased back into the leather sofa the bracelet dug into her hip bone. Her fingers plucked at the fold of fabric adjusting the hard sliver of the inscription plate so it didn't pinch into her so much. The bracelet was a constant reminder of the little girl.

But figuring out why she had been directed to find that bracelet was something that would have to wait.

Wait. Just like sitting there now waiting to see her mother and that specialist doctor.

***

A couple of hours later Paige looked up when a new doctor, an older guy in his mid-fifties, appeared at the side of her mother's bed.

His dark eyes flitted over to her, and he glanced at the chart in his hand before speaking. "You must be Paige, Mrs. Wright's daughter. I'm Dr. Bennett." He turned to gaze down at her mother and his eyes softened. "You had a pretty rough day yesterday, Cheryl. We've determined that a blood clot in the left hemisphere of your brain was the cause. A small section was affected. The anticoagulant which you were administered overnight has helped restore the flow. Even so, there were brain cells in the Broca area that died."

Paige had been hanging on every word while watching her mother's eyes. But with the doctor's latest sentence she interrupted, "But she'll recover all her faculties, won't she?"

He looked at her and smiled. "Given time and the right medication, I'm optimistic about that outcome. There's amazing plasticity in the brain. The surviving brain cells work overtime devising workarounds to help restore lost functionality. There is also medication to assist or stimulate the brain in this rewiring."

Tears glistened in Paige's eyes when she looked at her mother. "You're gonna be okay, Mom. Your brain is probably working on getting better right now."

The doctor tucked the clipboard under his arm and leaned closer to her mother. "Your speech is going to be affected judging from the area that was damaged. That's common and nothing to be unduly alarmed about, but you must have patience, Cheryl."

The other doctor, Dr. Morris, stepped into the room and stood next to Paige. The neurologist looked over at him. "We can transfer Mrs. Wright from ICU today. Schedule rehab to assess and recommend a therapy program. I'll check in on her in a couple of days and make a determination based on the team's assessment of her needs and the resources available if she can be released then."

Paige's heart leapt hearing that they were even thinking her mother may be able to go home in a couple of days. She squeezed her mother's hand and smiled seeing her mother's eyes close softly. There was even a small smile of relief when they opened, and Mom looked at her again.

She turned to the doctors who were about to leave, "Thanks. Just let me know what I can do. If it's hiring a nurse or home care to help me look after her, I'm all over that."

The younger doctor answered, "We'll know the best course

after the rest of the team has evaluated your mother."

They left the room, and Paige again turned to her mother. "Mom, this is going to work out." She looked down at her mother's worn hand. "I'm sorry I never visited you more. That's going to change, Mom. I promise."

FIFTEEN

It was almost ten at night when Paige arrived at her mother's house. It had been a long day but at least the anguish over her mother had eased. There were still lots of things she needed to do to support her, but knowing she'd get better made all the difference.

She glanced over at Karen's house and saw the light in the living room flickering from some program on TV. Karen had stayed at the hospital right up until dinner time before heading home.

Paige locked the car and walked up the narrow walkway, peering up when the motion light over the door flashed. Inside the house, as she was slipping her shoes off, she noticed a sliver of light peeking out from under the spare bedroom door. In her rush to get back to the hospital earlier, she must have left it on when she checked the house for intruders.

Flicking the hallway and kitchen lights on as she passed by, she entered the tiny bedroom. Long ago it had been converted into a sewing and craft room and now the small bed against the far wall was buried in an avalanche of totes, heaps of fabric and sewing supplies. Her mother's sewing table and machine rested against the wall closest to her, while the opposite one contained an old sea chest and a bookcase jammed with acrylic paints, magazines and even more brightly colored folded cloth.

She'd have to wait until her mother was home to make sure she wasn't going to pitch anything valuable out, but half of the crap in that room was definitely going. It was barely a cow path between the two walls with all the stuff crammed in there.

Paige smiled as she turned the light off and backed out of the room. If there *had* been an intruder earlier they could easily have hidden under some heap of stuff, and who would ever know? Hell. They may never be found again.

She wandered into the kitchen to make herself a cup of tea. A glass of wine would have been better, but there'd be no way her mother had any of that on hand. After filling the kettle with water, she pushed a collection of recipe books and a stack of junk mail to the side to make room on the counter. The electrical plug was easier to find, with the multiple cords hanging like the arms of an octopus from the outlet.

Leaning her backside against the countertop she looked around. There wasn't a horizontal surface that wasn't strewn with papers, knickknacks or plants. The room wasn't all that big but it looked even smaller because of the crowding. It was claustrophobic rather than homey. Her mother collected junk like a bee collected pollen. When she'd lived there she'd been able to keep a lid on her mother's obsession. But since she left home, Mom had really let loose.

She reached for a mug from the cabinet and rummaged for the tea bags. She had her choice of tea, from green to Irish Breakfast to chai. That was only the first layer visible. She grabbed the box of chai and plucked out a bag before shoving it back in the crowded space.

Her mother bordered on being a hoarder while Paige ascribed to minimalism. If she didn't use something for a couple months, out it went. Was this need for order something she'd inherited from her father's genes or was it a reaction to her mother's lifestyle? She loved her mother to pieces, but this mania to accumulate stuff had always bugged her.

When the kettle boiled she poured a cup and decided to

take it to her bedroom. It was either that or do battle with the coats and sweaters draped over the kitchen chairs to sit down.

As she passed by the sewing room she noticed that the light was once more seeping out from under the door. Her forehead knotted.

She'd turned that light out. What the hell?

She opened the door and looked at the wall switch. There was nothing on the wall next to it that could have jostled the switch—that in itself was odd considering the jumble of pictures competing for wall space. When she flicked the switch a few times, it wasn't like it was loose or anything. She took a deep breath and turned it off, before closing the door gently. Maybe she should call an electrician to check on it while she was staying there. If it was some kind of short then it could be a fire hazard.

She let out a yawn so deep she shuddered. That's it; time for bed.

She climbed into bed and booted up her laptop. She spent a while checking her email and got caught up on the news. The police still hadn't caught up with Cory Smith. Damn.

She snuggled under the patchwork quilt her mom had made for her. At least her job wasn't going to be a problem. Sheila had confirmed that she was clear for the next week at least in taking personal time to look after her mother. Thank God for Sheila. She could picture Bradley's scowl, operating the firm with just the two of them, having to turn away potential clients.

She set her laptop on the bedside table and then flicked the lamp off. Adjusting the pillows before settling in, her hand hit something hard. Her fingers glided over the small object and she froze. There was no need to turn the light on. She knew what her fingers felt.

Aubree's bracelet.

She pulled it out from under her pillow and sat up straight.

That bracelet should still be in her jeans where she'd left it. She hadn't given the bracelet a thought since that afternoon. Yet here it was tucked under her pillow. It was eerie as hell, but for some crazy reason she wasn't frightened this time. Not like that morning in the bathroom when it had appeared in her jeans.

Her gaze wandered over the room. "Aubree? You don't want me to forget you. That's it, isn't it?" She stayed still as a statue listening hard for any sound or sign. But only the faint tick of her mom's grandfather clock in the hallway could be heard.

She slid the bracelet back under her pillow and then laid her head down. "I won't forget you, Aubree. But I need to be here for my mom right now. I will go where you're leading me after that. Don't worry."

SIXTEEN

It was good to be able to sleep in the next morning. Her mother had been moved to another wing of the hospital and the duty nurse had told Paige to delay visiting until the afternoon. Apparently the rest of the team of medical specialists would be keeping her mom busy, each member assessing and making recommendations to speed recovery.

When Paige finally opened her eyes, the sun already well above the horizon, cast a warm honey glow on the footboard and across the room. A quick glance at her cell phone showed that it was almost ten o'clock. She sat up and threw the blankets back, stifling a yawn. It had been a while since she'd slept in that bed, seeing the dark limbs of the maple tree just outside her window. The only thing missing was her mom in the kitchen and the sound of plates and pans clattering.

She grabbed her robe from the back of the door and wandered down the hall to the bathroom. When she finished in there she paused, looking around the hallway at the jumble of stuff that lined the walls. She may not be able to throw things out, but at least she could organize and possibly box things up. Her mom might not be that steady on her feet, and having this junk crowding the way wouldn't help matters.

Picking up a magazine from the stack next to her she did an eye roll at the irony. Good Housekeeping.

She'd have a coffee and a bite to eat before tackling the heaps of junk. But as she was about to step into the kitchen a noise from the spare bedroom made her stop. It had been a click and then a low thud. She stepped over to the door and slowly turned the knob. Opening it an inch at a time, she peered into the room. Once more the overhead light was on, but there was nothing other than the usual debris on the floor. Nothing that could have made that thud when it fell.

The sea chest though. The lid was up and resting against the wall behind it. The hair on Paige's arms spiked high. That lid had been closed last night, and there was no one here but her. How had it lifted up like that? It was metal, weighing probably five pounds or more! That had been the thud—the lid banging against the wall when it opened.

She barely breathed staring hard at the sea chest. Her heart skipped a few beats in a mad rush as she peered at the chest.

How was that lid being open even possible? It had always been locked when she lived there. The realization dawned on her that this was the first time she'd seen it open. Ever. She remembered when she was a kid trying to pick the lock like she saw on TV shows. She tried a bunch of times until giving up. It had always worked on TV, but not for her.

And when Mom saw the scratches on the lock from her efforts…wow. She got really upset. Really, really upset. And not the yelling kind. No…it was worse. It was the sad upset. She sat Paige down and through teary eyes made her promise to never, ever, *ever* go into that chest.

Ever.

She wouldn't explain why, she just made Paige promise.

"I'll explain when you're a grown up, Paige," was all Mom had said about it.

Now, twenty years later, her mind was spinning with the guilt and apprehension of a twelve year old. Up until now, she had just decided that she'd respect Mom's privacy.

But with all that had been going on lately, curiosity

overwhelmed any sense of remorse as she peered down at the contents. *'What the hell, I'm grown up now, right?'* flitted through her mind. She knew she was making excuses, but maybe just a peek, okay?

The top layer was strewn with bundles of bank statements, each bundle with the year scrawled on the top envelope. Beside them were a stack of manila envelopes, each one also dated, but marked *Taxes* as well. Nestled into the mound of paperwork was a cardboard box with a clear plastic top. Inside she saw a cotton lace baby bonnet and christening gown, both yellowed with age.

She picked up the box and looked at the contents. That was *her* christening outfit. The box had been lying on a shallow wooden tray that was covering more stuff. She set the box aside and lifted the tray from the chest.

Her eyes opened wider seeing a collection of photo albums, scrapbooks and a thin black box. A quick rifle through the pages of the first album showed pictures of Paige from when she was a newborn to the first day of school. No doubt the other albums were more of the same.

But the box was bound with elastic that had hardened and split in a few places. It looked out of place in a chest devoted to capturing moments of Paige's life. The color, and the fact that the lid was secured, was curious.

A series of sharp raps made her jump.

Her eyes closed as she murmured to herself, "It's the front door. That's all," she said aloud to calm herself. Even so, her hands trembled from the surprise as she closed the chest and hurried down the hall.

When she opened the front door, Karen stood there. She smiled extending a plate. Waves of steam wafted from under the colorful napkin topping it. "Banana bread, fresh from the oven."

Paige opened the door wider, stepping back, "Come in! You shouldn't have, but it smells great." She took the plate from Karen and watched as the older woman shrugged out of a red fleece jacket.

Karen heaped it on top of another coat hanging on the rack and rubbed her hands together. "I put extra chocolate chips in it, just the way you like it."

Paige's mouth was already watering from the sweet aroma. "You spoil me, Karen." She led the way to the kitchen. "But that's why I love you! I was just about to make some coffee. This is perfect."

"I saw your car out front. I'm glad I caught you before you took off for the hospital. How was Cheryl after I left?" Karen asked as she sat down at the table.

Paige glanced over at Karen as she prepared the coffee. "She seemed pretty good all things considered. They're doing more tests and stuff with her this morning so I thought I'd sleep in."

"Good for you. You probably could use a good night's sleep after all this. First that dreadful murder and then your mother's illness."

All this. Karen was right; the past week had been hell on steroids. Paige got mugs down and then plates for the warm bread. She gazed at Karen as she took them over to the table. "I was beside myself when I heard about the murders. Actually I still am. But you want to know what's really weird?"

Karen looked up from where she was perched like a bird on the edge of the chair. "What? What's weird?"

"I met the mother in court...well not *met* exactly, but we spoke during the hearing. But after I learned of their deaths, I kept thinking of the *daughter*. I still do actually."

Taking a deep breath, she continued. "This may sound crazy but I swear I've seen the little girl a few times." Seeing Karen sit straighter, jerking back a little Paige wondered if she should have mentioned this. Karen would probably think she was totally losing it, seeing ghosts.

"What do you mean? How could you see her when she's dead?"

"It was just fleeting glimpses from the edge of my vision but it was *there*, Karen." She gulped and then kept going. "I even heard her voice on my cell phone."

"But Paige. That could have been the stress of it all. Your mind—"

"No. Hang on." Paige left the kitchen heading for her bedroom. She slid the bracelet out from under her pillow and brought it back with her. She held it out in front of Karen. "This bracelet was Aubree's. That was her name. I had dreams about a backyard with a swing and sandbox. It was so vivid. I could see the orange mums, the fenced yard and even the color of the house."

Karen could only stare up at her with wide eyes, her jaw falling open slowly.

Paige continued. "I went there, Karen. I know it's a macabre thing to do, but I had to go there. It was all exactly the way I'd dreamed it. *Exactly*. I found this partially buried in the sandbox. She wanted me to find it."

Karen got up and walked over to the counter to pour the coffee. Paige couldn't get a reading on what the older woman was thinking. "Karen? Do you believe me?" This woman was like a second mother. It was important that she understood.

Karen turned holding the mugs of coffee as she walked back to the table. "Of course I believe you. You've never lied to me or your mother. Not that I ever knew. But..." She blew out a long sigh as she set the mugs on the table and sat down. Looking up at Paige she continued. "I don't think it's healthy to hang on to that. Give it to the police. Maybe it will help them, or they can give it to the grandparents. You've got enough to worry about right now without getting mixed up in that murder."

Paige's eyes widened, and she blinked a few times staring at Karen. Of all the reactions she might have anticipated, this was the last thing she would have thought. Karen was warm and supportive normally—but *this?* Her words were cold. She was supposed to just wash the blood from her hands as if it didn't matter?

A child and her mother were dead because of her! She held her temper before it grew. Instead, she pulled out a chair and took a seat across from her godmother. "I can't do that, Karen.

Don't you see? As crazy as it sounds, Aubree is reaching out to me." She grit her teeth before exploding. "ME! Of all people, me. I don't know why, but I have to be open to this." She set her chin. "I'm going to run this down and follow where it leads."

Karen's eyes flashed. "Run it down, eh? Paige, you practice the law, not enforce it like a cop. Let the police handle this." She leaned into the younger woman. "You have more important things to do! You have to look after your mother! *That's* the important thing. Not go chasing after some stupid dreams." Karen shook her head and looked down. "The child is dead. You can't change that. This isn't helping you or your mother. Let it go."

SEVENTEEN

While Paige sat with her mother in the hospital, cory had his hands full dealing with a mother as well—except this one had whiskers and a black mask.

"Shit! That little fucker!" He peered at the bite on his ankle, gently touching the inflamed tissue. Even though he'd washed the wound and applied some antiseptic ointment, it looked red and puffy with infection. The ointment was probably expired. The old biddy who owned the cabin had probably bought it eons ago.

To make matters worse, he was down to his last hunk of wood for the stove. He'd have to go out and try to forage some more before the storm that was brewing hit. After applying a fresh bandage to his ankle he stood up and grabbed his jacket.

His eyes narrowed, relishing the weight of the knife in the pocket of the jacket. This time if that 'coon was around he'd inflict some serious damage, if not kill the bitch.

It wasn't bad enough that he was stuck in some rat-trap cabin in the middle of nowhere, but he'd probably get some kind of septic shock from the bite. His father was no help—three days since he'd seen him and supplies were running low.

Should I call him?

He blew out a fast sigh heading for the door. The old man would make fun of him and probably be pissed that he called. No, he'd wait another day and see if the swelling in his ankle went down.

The sky was gunmetal gray while the air was heavy with the threat of a downpour. He'd better hurry and get the wood. When he stepped into the growth of trees he peered at the spot where he'd had the encounter with the overgrown rodent. Part of him, a very large part if he was honest with himself, wished it would appear. He wouldn't kill it...not straight away. Just wound it—the same way the damned thing had made him suffer.

His foot nudged the heap of leaves and twigs where the baby raccoons had been. Nothing. The creature had probably moved on with whatever of her litter had survived. He turned away and spied through the underbrush for fallen tree limbs.

There was a maple tree about ten feet away that looked promising. A broken branch from the birch next to it was wedged in a fork of the lower limbs. At least it would be dry and not infested with bugs. As he made his way over there, a high-pitched scream brought him to a complete halt.

Once more, a howl pierced the air followed by rustling leaves and a thud coming from his left side. Eerily human sounding, there was also a catlike element. His hand shot into his pocket for the knife while he searched the area for any sign of movement.

A fleeting glimpse of silvery brown was soon hidden by the dying leaves of the underbrush. A lynx? He could have sworn he'd seen an ear topped with a pointed tuft of black. When it cried and hissed again, he knew he was right. There was a wild lynx in the woods with him! Shit!

His heart thudded quickly against his ribs as he raced out of the woods. A raccoon was one thing but a wildcat? He thought of the toms he'd hung from trees watching them squirm as they suffocated. Their talons had tried in vain to work the wire noose, often slicing their own necks in the process.

No way was he going to get into it with a fifty-pound cat. He grabbed the handle of the door and dove back inside the cabin. He needed a gun or an ax, not some two-bit pocketknife to do battle with the likes of that. Lynx were crazy fast and fierce.

He rushed to the window peering hard over at the stand of trees. Where was it? Movement to the right showed the lumbering grace of a lynx settling on a log. Slitted amber eyes watched the cabin, and seemed to be staring right at him.

Cory jerked back when a second cat joined the one sitting there. The new one was slightly smaller and had something in its mouth. It was hard to tell, but it looked like a squirrel when it dropped it next to the bigger cat. The two cats didn't look like they were in any kind of hurry to leave, but maybe the rain would change that.

He looked over at the supplies of food on the counter. There were a couple boxes of macaroni dinner and a can of baked beans. The wood wasn't the only thing he was low on. Somehow he had to get out to the road to see if there was a knapsack. The old man had promised to keep him supplied, and he'd damn well better have done that.

Once more he debated with himself whether a call to the old prick was in order.

With the two wildcats out there, a jaunt to the road only to find nothing wasn't something he was willing to risk. He grabbed the phone from the kitchen table.

After a few rings, his father answered. "What?"

Cory rolled his eyes. Not even a "hello," let alone a "how are you doing?" "I need supplies, but you're gonna have to drive to the cabin, not toss them near that post. There's wild animals—"

"I told you not to call me. Sit tight."

"Hey! You stuck me here! The least you can do is bring me supplies or maybe even a gun." When there was no response his forehead tightened. "Dad? Dad, are you there?"

A glance at the phone showed that his father had ended the call.

"Shit!" He flung the phone at the sofa where it bounced against a cushion. Threading his fingers through his hair he clenched his fists. "What the hell am I gonna do?"

He pulled the curtain back from the window and glanced up at the sky before searching the spot where the cats had been. They were gone now. And the rain still hadn't started. The woodstove showed only embers when he opened the heavy metal door. Pretty soon it would be freaking cold in the small cabin.

Gripping the wooden chair tucked into the table he lifted it high and then smashed it on the floor. It splintered into pieces, but one of the chair legs would make a decent club to stave off those cats if they were still out there. He should have grabbed a thick branch from the woods. But yesterday the only threat had been that stupid raccoon.

He stormed out the door with the chair leg in his fist. This was all Noele's fault. If she hadn't gone to the police and fought him in court, he wouldn't be stuck in some remote shack fighting wild animals. If she were here right now, he'd beat the shit out of her and the little brat. The kid looked more like Noele than him. He was more convinced than ever that the kid wasn't his. He wouldn't put anything past the two-bit whore.

"Hey cat! Come on out and fight me!" He could feel the vein in his forehead throb and even hear the beat of his heart. All the while his narrow eyes scanned the forest for any movement.

Bring it on! Every cell was firing with the adrenaline coursing through his body. The blinding rage had always been a high that was waaay better than sex. He was Rambo, an Avenger, a Transformer all rolled into one. Invincible.

He rushed at the woods with a lust for blood and revenge. First those cats and then that bitch raccoon.

What would raccoon meat taste like with a side of cat? He could almost feel the thud ripple through his arm muscles when he caught up with them. In his mind's eye he could see the spatter of blood and brains from a hard whack at their ugly heads.

A low growl to his right made him spin in that direction. At the scratching of claws and the crack of tree limbs breaking, he spied movement in the dark oak ten feet away. Both cats clung to the trunk, making their way higher as he raced toward it.

He swung the chair leg against the tree, glaring up into the bigger cat's eyes. "C'mon down, mister kitty. I'll show you a thing or two about fighting."

The cat growled and hissed at him.

Cory spied a fist-sized rock and backing slowly away, he hurled it high at the cat, missing it by a few inches. The other cat slithered higher, rounding the trunk until it was out of sight.

"Ha! I'll get you, cat." Cory rummaged around the floor of the forest searching for more rocks. This was more fun than shooting fish in a barrel.

EIGHTEEN

Michael Smith slid the cheap burner phone into the pocket of his sports jacket. His heart beat faster as he peered through the door opening at the reception room. There was only Marcy there, sitting at her desk typing and staring at her computer monitor. It didn't look like she'd heard any of the call from Cory.

That bloody fool! He was told not to call unless it was an emergency. Michael rose from his desk and darted over to the window overlooking the parking lot and the street. Nothing unusual in the lot. All the cars there belonged to his salespeople, and of course there was Marcy's beater. But that black Buick was parked on the street...for the second day. An unmarked police car?

Had they believed him when they barged into his office and grilled him? Probably not. Why else would they question his neighbor? But good old Bob had backed him up. He'd been happy to report that "he hadn't seen hide nor hair of Cory visiting his dad in many, many years."

But still there was that black Buick.

When Cory had showed up at three in the morning that Saturday night, he should have told him to get lost. The last thing he needed was cops nosing around his home and business.

His slate wasn't exactly lily white, and there was no need to bring *that* to light. As far as his staff and the business community were concerned, he was an upstanding businessman, if not a civic leader. Hell, people even showed sympathy for him after Lorraine left him. Poor man, raising their son all on his own.

He turned away from the window and went back to his desk, flopping heavily into the leather chair. That stupid kid. But he was his son, dammit. He'd done the best he could with the boy.

How many fathers turned a blind eye to their kid's antics. Getting in fights was normal enough. But Cory had bullied and beat that crippled Graham kid so much that the parents threatened to sue. The kid had been a loser just like his old man. Cory having a hate-on for him was...well it was understandable. But he'd gotten caught. That was unforgivable.

At least with the neighborhood cats, he'd been a little more discreet.

But this. Killing his wife and daughter? The woman had been an immigrant so she didn't count but the little girl? That was his own flesh and blood. He'd only held his granddaughter once after she was born. Cory should have taken the offer of a job and house in Poughkeepsie rather than totally lose his shit. Some family reunion that had been.

He rolled his eyes at the memory. He had sucked it up and lined up a job for the boy. A hell of a lot better one than what he had going on at that stupid nightclub. But no…the kid had started in on him as soon as he realized that Dad wasn't bringing in a fat check, just a job offer.

From there things got even louder. The neighbors in that shitty subdivision had called the cops and that ended his relationship with his son.

And now the kid was back asking for his help.

Michael sat back in his chair and folded his hands across his belly.

Fuck 'im.

If the cops dug up any dirt about his own past, the kid was toast. If anything from his own past came back to haunt him, he'd cut a deal and turn Cory in so fast it'd make their heads spin.

He snorted, finally admitting to himself that stashing Cory wasn't so much looking after his boy as maintaining an insurance policy.

It was survival of the fittest, and it was beginning to look like his son wasn't gonna make it.

NINETEEN

Later that night Paige arrived back at her mother's house and found a piece of paper wedged into the crack of the doorframe. She plucked it from the spot and unfolded it, holding it under the glow of the overhead light.

Hi Paige. I heard from Jenny that your mom is sick. I would have called you, but I lost all my contacts when my cell phone took a swim in the toilet. Call me when you get in. I'd love to see you! If there's anything I can do for you or your mother, I'm here.

555 577 6732

Hannah

She smiled seeing Hannah's hand-drawn sad-face emoji. Of all the friends she'd made while living in the small town, Hannah was the only one who made a real effort, trying to stay in touch. She was the center of the hub, passing along updates of the gang of friends who had scattered across the country like dandelion fluff.

Maybe in a day or so, once her mother was home again,

she'd give Hannah a call to catch up. Paige entered the house and locked the door behind her. As she was hanging up her jacket she noticed the light creeping out from under the spare room again.

Her eyes squinted as she traced her actions before she'd left the house. Karen had stayed until almost noon. After she'd left, it had been a mad rush to get ready to get back to the hospital. There was no way she'd gone into that spare room. She distinctly recalled turning the light off and closing the door there shortly after she'd got up.

Yet the light was on in there, once again.

She walked down the hallway and opened the door. Her gaze immediately flew to the sea chest. Again it was open, the lid resting against the wall. A shiver skittered up her spine as she stood peering at it. That had definitely been closed when she'd left the room. She remembered feeling guilty looking into it. She'd been invading her mother's privacy; there was no getting around that fact.

"What the heck is going on here?" she whispered as she scanned the rest of the room. She cocked an ear, almost expecting a reply. Something very odd was happening in that room. The chest…

She was hardly aware of wandering over and kneeling before it.

As she was about to, once more, lift the top tray out, she paused. This was wrong. Going through and sorting her mother's things in the other rooms was one thing, but this... It was nothing more than snooping into her mother's private affairs. She was taking advantage of the fact that her mother wasn't here and that the box wasn't locked.

She pulled the lid shut and then, for good measure, she set one of the heavy craft bins on top. It would take an enormous effort to lift the lid now. With a roll of her eyes she rose to her feet. It shouldn't have opened in the first place, not all by itself.

But had she left it open that morning? It was the only reasonable explanation. But so much had been happening that defied logic. She pulled her cell phone from her pocket and snapped a picture of the chest shut tight with the bin anchoring it.

There. The photo was time stamped and proof that she'd shut it. If that lid opened again she'd seriously consider moving it to the basement. This was altogether too creepy for words.

She went into the kitchen and plugged the kettle in. As she waited for it to boil to make a cup of tea, she started the task of tidying up. Sweaters hanging from the backs of chairs were swept up into her arms and toted to her mother's bedroom. When she opened the closet a new set of problems met her. There was no room for even one more item!

Tossing the sweaters onto the heap of clothes stacked on an easy chair, Paige threw her hands in the air. How could her mother live like this? It was small wonder with the jumble of "stuff," that the woman had suffered a stroke. Hell. It was hard to breathe, let alone move around in there.

As fast as the balloon of anger filled her chest it popped when a wave of guilt flooded through her. Her mother was sick. And not just physically. Hanging on to clothes, old pictures and even outdated magazines was a sickness. Her mother was a hoarder. This wasn't going to be solved with a visit to the town's dump. It was a problem that had to be carefully tackled. That is if she didn't want to risk her mother stroking out again.

She trudged back to the kitchen and unplugged the kettle. As she waited for the tea bag to steep, she looked at her phone, checking email and any news item. Nothing there about Cory, and the few emails from her friends at the office could wait. She was about to set it down when her thumb must have touched the photo app. A picture of the trunk and the heavy green bin flashed before her eyes. But that was not all. Instead of the butter cream wall there was a hazy bluish glow above the bin. Her fingers flicked increasing the size of the photo, moving it to center on the glow.

Her eyes became wide searching the blurred area above the bin. Everything else about the picture was sharp, even showing a line of rust near the latch of the chest. That haze hovering above confirmed her darkest fear. There was nothing wrong with her memory. It was the chest. There was some kind of spirit attached to it that she'd caught a glimpse of in the camera lens.

First the visions and dreams of the little girl and now this? In the house she'd grown up in! What the hell was happening to her? Shit! It was like she'd become some kind of psychic or something. The paranormal was becoming the norm.

None of this should be happening. But it was. And it had all started when Aubree and Noele were murdered. Somehow, some way she had to help the little girl. She'd had every intention of doing that, but this stuff happening in her mother's house underscored the urgency. There would be no peace in her life until the girl's murderer was found.

Goddamn it! She wiped her eyes. Every single goddamned time she so much as *thought* of Aubree, she started blubbering! She had cried more in the last few days than she had in her entire life!

She took the bracelet from her pocket and held it up, gazing at it through tears. "I'm going to help you. But my mom needs me too. Just give me some time, will you?"

But that haze over the chest kept niggling in the back of her mind. She walked across the kitchen and peered down the hallway to the spare room. Again the crack of light flowed out into the hallway from under the door. She sighed and threaded her fingers through her hair. She had definitely turned that light off when she'd left the room.

C'mon, Aubree! Gimme a break!

Should she open the chest again and see what could be in there? Maybe if she did all this spookiness with the chest would stop.

But her mother's face flitted over her mind's eye. She would be hurt and probably angry. Plus, if Paige went through her stuff, she'd know. It was part of the reason that Paige had never lied to her. Her mother had some kind of sixth sense when it came to Paige trying to hide something from her.

The woman was sick enough as it was. Finding that Paige

had gone through her private stuff might set her back. Or worse.

She couldn't take that chance. In the meantime, she'd have to put up with this.

She ground her teeth in frustration. Goddamn it!

TWENTY

Two days later...

"Well, Mom, welcome home," Paige said, opening the front door with a flourish.

When Cheryl entered the house she stopped dead in her tracks and gaped at her daughter. There was fire in her eyes while her mouth and brain warred trying to form words.

But Paige was prepared for this. "Mom! I didn't throw your stuff out. It's boxed up. We can go through it together to see what you need to keep." She helped her mother out of her coat and hung it up. She'd even sorted through the jumble of scarves, jackets and coats, getting them put away in a spare closet. The hallway floor was actually visible now, replete with a good coat of wax on the hardwood.

In a rush she continued. "Seriously. I was worried about you getting around with all the stuff you have clogging the hallway. The last thing you need is to fall and break your arm or something." Paige tried to soften her next words, seeing the look of hurt appear in her mother's eyes. "I wouldn't throw anything away without your say so, Mom."

Karen stepped into the entryway behind Paige. "I've got a chicken casserole in the oven, Cheryl. You must be sick of hospital food by now."

Cheryl managed a smile and a quick nod of her head, looking at Karen. "Y...yes."

Paige's eyebrows shot up, and she gripped her mother's arm. "Mom! You spoke! That's after only one therapy session. Imagine how well you'll do after a week or so."

Her mother's eyes blinked a few times. Struggling slightly, she repeated, "Yes."

Karen slipped by Paige and gave her friend a one-armed hug, "You're going to be all right, sweetie."

Paige swallowed the lump in her throat seeing the bond between the two women. If not for that bond, things might easily have been much worse. Karen had spent almost as much time visiting her mother in the hospital as she had.

"Mom? Do you want to take a nap before we have dinner? It's still early."

Karen chimed in as well. "That's a good idea, Cheryl. You don't want to overwhelm yourself." She glanced at Paige. "The same goes for you, Paige. Go out for a walk or visit one of your friends. You've been at that hospital for four days steady. I'll get your mother settled."

The prospect of being alone for even an hour knowing her mother was in good hands was a welcome reprieve. She'd been a ball of nerves, flitting to the hospital, organizing the house, all the while pushing the thought of Aubree and that damned chest to the far recesses of her mind. She'd been tempted to move it to the basement, and it was only the sheer weight of it that prevented her.

A walk to the shoreline, watching the swell of waves had always been therapeutic when she'd lived in the small town of Madison. She could use a walk to clear her head.

"Are you sure, Karen?"

But it was her mother who replied, "G...g...go." She took a deep breath and smiled, proud that she'd managed to retrieve the word.

"Okay. I'll go! I can take a hint." Paige gave her mother's cheek a kiss. "I'll only be an hour or so. Call me if you need me."

She headed out the door and paused on the front step inhaling deeply. The smell of burning leaves drifted in the air, and a column of smoke rose above the roofline of the house across the street. Old Mr. Crane was almost seventy, but he still carried on with yard work, clearing his garden and burning the refuse. It brought back bittersweet memories of life in the seaside town.

Although she never understood why her mother had chosen to live in Madison, she was glad she had. The beach overlooking the Long Island Sound was only a ten-minute walk from her house. How many beach parties had she enjoyed there with the gang? She should probably give Hannah a call, but for now, the solitude of a walk to the shore was more appealing.

Her hand slipped into her pocket, and once more she looked at the child's bracelet. Aubree would never know the joys of growing up, tossing pebbles into the surf with friends, seeing sunsets dance gold and orange ribbons on the waves. Even walking along streets she'd walked a thousand times, the child's memory haunted her.

As she was about to cross the street and cut through to the walkway leading to the ocean, a red sports car came screeching to a halt next to her. She jerked back seeing the door pop open and a willowy blonde step out.

The woman strode over to Paige, practically yelling, "Aubree! Just who the hell is Aubree, and why didn't you call me when you got in?" The blonde woman yanked her dark sunglasses off and glared at Paige.

TWENTY ONE

OH. MY. GOD.

Paige could only stare. Of course it was Melanie, but at the same time...what had happened to the sweet demure girl she'd hung out with? Melanie had blown past assertion going straight to aggression.

"Melanie? What the—"

"First off, how's your mother?" Melanie gripped Paige's shoulders giving her a little shake.

Paige was still reeling seeing the fire in Melanie's eyes, the expensive leather coat and tight jeans topping spiked-heeled boots. She was even wearing makeup, and her hair was a crafted mess of toppled curls! This wasn't the same Melanie Walker who'd always been a chameleon blending into the background.

To say nothing of the fact that it had been years since she'd talked to Melanie. Yet, here she was giving Paige the third degree! And how did she know about Aubree?

Paige's face tightened, and she blared right back at her friend. "Mom's fine! Well, not fine but she will be! And what do you know about Aubree? How the hell—"

"I *dream* about her every night—a little girl playing in a

sandbox! What the hell? But the really weird thing is that *you're* there too!" Melanie stepped back, and for the first time she folded into herself, the way she always had. She even chewed at the cuticle of her thumbnail, staring down at the sidewalk. This was the Melanie that Paige knew.

But how was it possible that Melanie was involved in this too? The same dreams?

Paige thrust the bracelet in front of her friend's face. Melanie didn't need to say anything; the horror in her eyes said it all.

"That's *hers*. How did you get this?" Melanie pulled her shoulders back, her eyes now hard and glittering. She tried to take it from Paige, but her fingers only clawed at Paige's sleeve. "Give it to me!"

"No!"

"Let me see it, dammit!" Melanie reached around Paige's back, scrabbling at the bracelet. Paige held it up as high as she could while shoving the woman back.

"No! It's mine. You're not having it!"

Melanie made one last swipe of her hand, but Paige held it high. Considering that Paige was almost six feet tall while Melanie barely topped five three, it was a no brainer. There was no way Mel was getting it.

Melanie stopped her clawing and crossed her arms. "Goddamn it, Paige! You're acting like Golem in Lord of the Freaking Rings! I swear to God, if you say 'precious,' I'm gonna brain you!"

Paige's mouth hung open in shock, and then she laughed lightly. Still keeping her distance, she said, "Melanie, I had those same dreams. I went to her house and found this." Paige felt tears stinging the backs of her eyes, and she took a deep breath to avoid breaking down in front of her friend. "I know why I had those dreams, but what I don't get is why *you're* dreaming of her. How are you connected? Were you in Albany? We need to talk. C'mon." She grabbed the sleeve of Melanie's jacket and tugged her along, crossing the street.

Melanie yanked her arm away but kept up the fast stride

alongside Paige, her heels clacking on the asphalt. "Why didn't you answer my calls? I went through some serious shit a few years back. I tried to contact you, left tons of messages. What the hell happened to you? You just vanished off the face of the earth? We were friends. At least I thought we were."

Paige's chest sunk lower. It was true. Melanie had left messages. "Wait a damn minute; I did return your call!"

"Yeah, once, and you left a voice mail. I called back, and left you a voice mail." Melanie turned her hands over each other as she continued. "Then I left you another. And another…" She stopped and stared at Paige. "Until I realized you *didn't* want to hear from me."

Paige sighed. "It wasn't that; I was busy!"

"Oh for the love of God…" Melanie made finger quotes. *"That busy?"*

"Yes, actually." Paige held out a finger. "First of all, I was working a full-time job while also studying for the bar." She stabbed a finger in the air. "I was a walking zombie for most of that time, functioning on five hours of sleep a day."

"Yeah, but—"

Paige cut her off with a chopping motion. "But nothing! It was tough! And now..." She sighed. "Let me tell you, working at my firm makes all the stuff before that look like a part-time job! I'm in the office *at least* seventy goddamn hours a freaking week!" She looked around her old neighborhood and her voice grew quiet. "Since Aubree died and now my mom…this is the first time in *four years* I've had more than two days off in a row!"

Melanie chewed her lip. "Hey…"

"So, yeah, Melanie…" Paige's voice softened. "I've really, really been *busy*, okay?"

Melanie closed and opened her eyes. "Okay."

Paige looked over at her friend. "I'm sorry, Mel. Maybe I should have tried harder or something. I didn't realize how badly you needed me, okay? I dropped the ball. I'm really sorry." Her face tightened. "What happened? What shit did you go through?"

Melanie barked a short laugh. "Oh, nothing serious. Just getting possessed by a demon, almost killing my college friends at some haunted resort. But hey! It was all worth it. I inherited ten million dollars!" She crossed her arms and made a cheese grin. "How's that for idle chitchat, catching up?"

Paige stopped dead in her tracks. Gripping Melanie's arm, she gaped at her. "What? Are you kidding me? You were *possessed*? Mel, how much weed do you smoke these days?"

Melanie fluttered her hand in dismissal as she pulled away from Paige. "I don't do weed anymore. It's all true. My life changed after that weekend. And frankly, I resent the hell out of getting mixed up with anything supernatural again. I don't need that shit, but the dreams are getting worse."

Paige stepped off the boardwalk and onto the sand. When she saw that Melanie wasn't next to her she turned to see her friend with hands on hips, still on the wooden walkway.

"What? I'm not plowing through that sand in these boots. No. Way."

Paige rolled her eyes and stomped back to her. "When did you start dressing like a runway model? This is Madison not the Big Apple."

"These boots are Gucci and so's my jacket! My life became a total do-over after that weekend in the Catskills." Melanie scraped her fingers through her hair, "But now these damned dreams! I can't help that little girl, so why is she haunting me? And why would you be there with her? There's no way you can dodge me like you've been doing these past few years. I had to see you. This has got to stop before I lose my mind."

Paige jerked back. "I wasn't *dodging* you! Well, not on purpose. It's just the way it worked out." She shook her head thinking about how she'd been so involved in her own life. She'd lost touch with Mel and all her friends. Not to mention how she hadn't visited her mother nearly enough. And then the poor woman had a stroke.

No. She's lying to herself. The truth was that she'd become too caught up in her own ambitions. What kind of person had she become?

"Hey! Earth to Paige! The dreams. The little girl, and you being in my dreams. Care to enlighten me?"

Paige was jolted back at Melanie's words, shot out like bullets. "We need to talk. Let's get a coffee. We can try to figure this out."

"Make it whisky and I'm in!"

Paige stared at Melanie, trying to decide if she even *liked* this version of her friend. Flashy clothes and car, snarky attitude. That had to have been some weekend! "Okay. But you're buying, Miss Fancy Pants. I think you can afford it. Was that actually a Ferrari you pulled up in?"

Melanie grinned. "With all the bells and whistles! I'm loaded. I've got the house here, a condo in LA, and a time-share in France!" Her smile fell, and she looked over at Paige. "Now tell me about this little girl. What's the connection to you? Who is she?"

Paige took a deep breath, looking up the street to the flashing lights of a small pub and tavern. "I'll explain everything. Let's go to the Crown and Pint. After all that's happened, I could use a drink too."

The two women entered the warmth of the small room where a bartender stood polishing glasses behind an ancient oak bar. A couple guys in business suits sat at the far end, probably stopping for a drink before heading home from work. Paige led the way to an empty table next to the window.

When they were settled, a waitress arrived and handed them menus.

Paige held up her hand. "Just a drink, please. Two Jack Daniels and soda."

Melanie chirped, "Make mine a double with lots of ice." When the woman left, she turned once more to Paige. "Okay. Start at the top. I want to know about this kid. Don't get me wrong. I still want to hear what's been going in your life, but I need to know about the little girl. Maybe then I'll be able to get a decent night's sleep."

Paige sighed. "I practice the law, Mel—family law, specifically. I represented Cory Smith in court to allow him access to his daughter, Aubree. I'm pretty sure he killed her and his ex-wife. The police are after him but he's disappeared." She let out a long sigh. "The little girl in your dreams is Aubree."

Melanie sat back allowing the waitress to set the two drinks down on the table. When she left, Melanie stared at Paige, "There was something in the paper about some guy murdering his wife and kid, but that was up in Albany. I didn't bother reading it."

Paige nodded. "Yeah, that's the one."

Melanie's eyes widened. "That was *you* who represented him and gave him access? Oh my God. You must feel like shit about that."

"That's a serious understatement. If I could do it over—"

"You can't, so don't go down that road, Paige. You also don't have a crystal ball. You didn't know what would happen. It totally sucks but that's life." She sighed cupping the glass of whisky between her hands. "But these dreams… you're having them too?" Melanie hunched over the table, peering into Paige's eyes.

"Yeah. And not just dreams. This may be hard to believe, but I started seeing her everywhere." She took a deep breath and continued. "She even left a message on my phone. But I was totally floored when I went to her house."

"It's dark yellow with burgundy shutters, right?" Melanie took a sip of her drink and set the glass down with a sharp thud. "I believe you, Paige. After what I've been through I'll believe anything when it comes to the afterlife." Her eyes became hard, looking at Paige. "I don't want to have anything more to do with this stuff, but it looks like I'm being pulled down this shitty rabbit hole again."

Paige could only stare at her friend silently. Melanie had a sharp edge that had never been there when they were growing up. She'd changed a LOT. It must have been a nightmare what happened to her. Yet here she was trying to figure this out and offer help.

"What happened to you, Mel? You're so different than when I last saw you."

Melanie looked down staring into her drink for a few moments. "That weekend... It was like something out of a horror movie. I thought I had an understanding about paranormal things...you know, the Ouija board and séances..." She made a small wave with her hand and with a rueful smile added, "We had some scary slumber parties as kids, right?"

Paige couldn't help but smile too. "We sure did." She tilted her head. "But that was then. What happened?"

Melanie shrugged. "I've always been interested in the paranormal. Nothing huge, but you know, I'd read some books and looked at stuff online…" Her voice trailed off. "But then…"

Paige let the silence hang. Mel would get to it.

Melanie took a deep breath. "I made really good friends in college. The four of us…we stayed in touch; every year after we graduated, we'd have a weekend get-together." Her mouth turned down. "But…a year and a half ago, Dara died."

"Who's Dara?"

"She was one of us. It was me, Becky, Cindy…and Dara. After she died, her will required us to spend a weekend at a place she owned." Melanie shuddered. "It was horrible." Lifting her eyes, she stared into Paige's eyes, "I just wanted to reconnect with a dear friend who'd died. And I did!"

"What, you communicated with your dead friend?"

"Yeah…but there are dark forces out there, too, Paige. And they *used* me. My obsession with the afterlife was the chink they used to control me. It was bad, Paige! I was fucking mind-raped by them!"

"What!" Paige didn't even know what that meant.

"That…*thing* took me over! It made me…" Melanie's face twisted at the memory. "It made me *hate* with such fury! I hated everyone!" Her face relaxed, and with wonder, and her voice almost a whisper, she added, "I almost killed my two other friends who were there."

"You're shitting me." A shock of fear spiked through Paige; Melanie was telling the truth.

"No, I'm not." She shot Paige a look. "And right now, I know that you know I'm telling the truth." Silence hung for a moment. Melanie took another deep breath. "I got through it. I've been through psychotherapy"—she paused and her voice became a low whisper—"and exorcisms. Many exorcisms."

Paige could only stare at Melanie silently for a few moments. Exorcisms? Melanie had never been much of a churchgoer. Whatever had happened had affected her so much that she'd turned to the church. And she couldn't deny that Melanie was a changed person.

"You were really possessed? Honestly, I've never believed in all that, but—"

"It's real. Trust me. I've experienced it. I was lucky to get through it. If not for some pretty special people, I might not have." She grit her teeth, shaking her head a little. "Having any more contact with the afterlife is the last thing I ever want to go through." She clenched her fists. "But these dreams of Aubree. And you. What the hell?"

Paige could see that Melanie was fighting back tears, her voice cracking when she spoke. She reached across the table and squeezed Melanie's hand. "I'm so very sorry I never tried harder to get in touch with you. If I'd known, maybe—"

"There was nothing you could have done. But I wanted to talk to you. I think I was trying to reconnect with who I was. I mean, we grew up together. You knew me better than my own mother."

Now it was Paige who fought tears, her throat closing up. "God, I feel terrible, Mel. Can I ever make it up to you?"

Melanie swiped at the tear that spilled down her cheek and smiled. "If you can make these damned dreams go away, that'd be a good start."

"I'll try." Paige paused for a few beats trying to figure out where to start after Melanie's story. The poor woman had been through hell from the sound of it. She really wanted to distance herself from these kinds of inexplicable events, but there was no other way to tackle this. She had to be completely honest about what was going on.

She gave Melanie the rundown of what the last few days have been like. The news of Aubree's murder, the apparitions, that insane voice mail. Then everything being thrown into chaos with her mother's stroke and her return to Connecticut.

Taking a deep breath, Paige continued. "I've even had some weird stuff happen at Mom's house too. The light in the spare room keeps coming on, even though I know I turned it off. That's happened a bunch of times. And then there's this old sea chest in her sewing room. It keeps opening on its own, and—"

"What's in the chest? It has to be connected to this, don't you think? Have you looked through it?"

Paige pulled back and shook her head. "No! I can't. All the time growing up Mom kept it locked. She's got personal stuff, private stuff in there. It would be wrong to go through her stuff."

Melanie's eyebrows flew up. "What? You're kidding me, right? With all the spooky shit going on, you're more interested in respecting your mother's privacy than checking it out? Paige…" She shook her head and looked down into her drink.

Paige could feel her jaw tighten. "For God's sake, Mel. My mom had a stroke! You think I'd risk upsetting her by snooping in her stuff? I couldn't do that. If I was responsible for her getting sick again, I'd never forgive myself. Plus we don't know for sure that it has anything to do with Aubree."

Melanie did an eye roll. "Seriously? Of *course* it's connected! You're wussing out, Paige. You know it, and so do I." She took another long sip of her drink, and when she looked over at Paige her features softened. "Look, I get that you feel bad about your mother's stroke. You probably even feel a bit guilty because you weren't around more. But seeing what's in that chest is more important right now than your sensitivity to your mother's privacy."

Her eyes glinted when she grinned. "Which is why I'm going to go through that chest."

"No you aren't! You can't—"

Melanie slapped the tabletop, hard enough that the drinks jostled. "I haven't had a decent night's sleep in almost a week! Like it or not, I'm in this with you, girlfriend! There's got to be some connection between the dreams and what's going on in your house with that chest. I promise if I find something really personal like sex toys or something I'll never breathe a word. But I've got to check it out even if you don't want to."

Sex toys? Eeew. Who was this woman, talking about sex toys in the same breath as Mom? But she could tell that Melanie was totally serious. Paige's eyes narrowed. "You won't find anything like that. Trust me. But maybe it wouldn't hurt to take a peek."

Melanie was right, and this was the only way to tackle this. That box secured by the elastic band was curious. If there was some connection to Aubree, Melanie would find it. She trusted Mel to be discreet if it was anything that would embarrass her mother.

"Hey! I was teasing about the sex toys. But there's got to be something…"

Paige swallowed hard. "There may be something. I did kind of peek into the chest. There was a box that she'd hidden in the lower level under my christening gown."

"Aha! So you *did* snoop! I knew it!" Melanie chuckled and then took a long swallow of whisky, polishing it off.

"I didn't snoop! I put everything back and never opened that black box."

Melanie signaled to the waitress to bring another round, and then her smile dropped gazing at Paige. "Aubree wants me to help you. That much should be clear to both of us. We're supposed to work together to find her killer."

"Good luck with that. The police can't even find him." Paige took a deep breath. "Can you believe that this is even happening? These dreams, that chest? Now we're following a dead girl's directions. I never believed in this kind of paranormal crap."

"There are more things in heaven and earth, Horatio, than are dreamt of in your philosophy."

Paige smiled. "Shakespeare. Tenth grade. Mrs. McCarthy would be proud, Mel."

Melanie smiled and passed a fifty dollar bill to the waitress when she appeared with the drinks. She waved at her to keep the change and turned back to Paige. There was a grim set to her mouth. "You should get back to your mom. Tell her I'll come over to see her tomorrow."

Paige took a long sip of the Jack Daniels relishing the slow burn in her belly. For once the muscles in the back of her neck seemed to loosen in the warmth of the whisky. "You'll go through her chest when you visit, right? Wait till she's asleep at least."

"Absolutely! And trust me, Paige. I'll keep her secrets if I don't think we need to know them. But we have to do this. There has to be something there."

Paige finished her drink and slipped her jacket on. "Are you still on Sycamore Avenue? You'd better walk home or take a cab."

"Not to worry. Seth will come and pick me up."

Seeing Paige's jaw drop, she added, "We've got some catching up to do, girlfriend. After we help Aubree."

TWENTY TWO

Later that night Paige sat with her mother in the living room. Karen had helped clean up after a wonderful dinner and had left. The TV was playing some sitcom but it was more background noise than anything either of them paid any attention to. Still, it brought back memories of times they'd shared not talking much but content with just being with each other.

Paige felt her mother's hand slip over hers. The two of them were sharing an afghan that Cheryl had crocheted. It was cozy and nice. No thoughts of Aubree or the strange sea chest.

"Would you like some tea or hot chocolate, Mom?" Paige looked into her mother's face, noting the lines that had deepened in her forehead. It was the only thing that had changed about her mother's face. Her sky-blue eyes still sparkled even if there were worn cusps of darker flesh under them.

Her mother shook her head and squeezed Paige's hand. It was enough to just be there, sharing the moment.

Paige smiled. "I ran into Melanie Walker earlier. She wants to visit you tomorrow. You won't believe how she's changed, Mom. She's not the mousy girl she used to be. I'm just giving you a heads up because she knocked me for a loop."

Her mother nodded, and her lips moved silently until the word she was seeking popped out. "Good. Melanie. Y...yes."

Paige breathed out a sigh of relief when the words her mother had obviously struggled with came out. She glanced at the television set and then grabbed the remote, turning it off. Her mother's eyes widened when Paige got to her feet.

"Hang on, Mom. I've got an idea." She raced into the bedroom and picked her laptop from the dresser. When she settled again with her mother, she clicked the pictures folder and watched it open showing a series of icons. Some of the photos were older, taken mostly during holidays she had shared with her mother.

The screen filled with a photo of her mother and her eating ice cream cones in Olin Park. Paige tilted the screen so her mother could have a better look. "Remember that day, Mom? It was the Fourth of July and we staked a spot to watch the fireworks later." She nudged her mother's arm. "You told me to get vanilla ice cream, that wearing a white T-shirt and picking chocolate was tempting fate. You were right from the looks of that stain."

Aside from the fond memories she knew her mother would enjoy, it was the elements in the photos that Paige wanted to subtly mention.

She brushed the screen to a picture of her mother on her hands and knees weeding her flower bed while a neighbor's dog was squatting at the edge of the lawn, leaving a stinky present.

"I wonder if the Joneses ever got another dog after Barney died. Your petunias looked really nice that year, Mom."

The speech therapist had recommended a touch-screen tablet and a program which her mother could use to help her recover her speech. She'd buy one the next day and set things up, but in the meantime, sharing memories while saying the names of different items in the pictures would help her mother's therapy.

The smile in her mother's eyes as they thumbed through

the photos was a reward in itself, but when Cheryl managed to repeat a few words, Paige's chest filled with joy. Mom would be visiting the speech clinic a couple times a week for the afternoon, but it was important to support the efforts of rehabilitation.

An hour passed like it was just ten minutes, the two of them sitting close in the dim room while the screen glowed with colorful pictures. They were nearing the end of the photo file when the screen went black.

Immediately it flashed back on, showing the same school picture of Aubree that had appeared in the news reports. Her mother jerked back, her mouth working to find words. Paige clicked the mouse, hit the escape key and even tried shutting the laptop down but still the screen showed the cheery little girl missing a front tooth in a lopsided smile.

The laptop had frozen. Paige's heart leapt into overdrive seeing the haunting image. How the hell…

She looked over at her mother. The alarm in her mother's face shot a bolt of fear through her chest. It wasn't just that that image had just shown up out of the blue. There was more to it.

"You know about this girl? Aubree Smith?" She peered into her mother's eyes.

Her mother nodded and then pushed the laptop off to the side. Her hands rose to cover her face.

Paige looked at the laptop, now showing just a dark screen. That shouldn't have happened! It wasn't the news article, it was *just* Aubree's photo!

'Dammit, Aubree! That's not fair. Pick on me all you want, but my mom had a stroke for God's sake!' Paige's annoyance with Aubree faded quickly; the child had been murdered. But still… it wasn't fair.

She looked over to her mother. Of course Mom must have heard the news about the murders the day she had the stroke. The poor woman had tears in her eyes as she tried to get up. That photo really shook her up.

"Mom. Wait. Let me help you." Paige rose and held her

mother's elbow walking her to her bedroom. A couple times her mother faltered in her step. This had upset her more than Paige would have thought. But her mother was a softhearted person. Still…

Paige wasn't sure who she was trying to comfort more, herself or Mom, when she spoke. "My computer has been acting strange. I'm going to have it looked at when I get your tablet."

When her mother paused beside her, Paige looked over to see her mouth moving but no words coming out. Her face was flushed and her eyes squeezed tight in frustration.

"It's okay, Mom. I'll get you settled in bed and then if you want, I can get a pen and paper. Don't worry that you can't say the words. Maybe you can write them, okay?" Her mother's eyes closed for a few beats and she nodded.

They passed the spare bedroom at the end of the hall. Paige wasn't surprised to see the light once more peeking out from under the door. But her mother didn't seem to notice, which was just as well. The poor woman was upset enough as it was.

Any thought she'd had of telling her mother that she had played a part in the murder by representing Cory, vanished. Her mother wasn't strong enough for that. Especially considering what she'd just seen, the turn in her behavior when that photo had popped onto the screen.

She helped her mother undress and get a nightgown on, all the while singing softly, "You are my sunshine, my only sunshine. You make me happy when skies are gray." It was the song that Mom used to sing to Paige when she was a little girl getting ready for bed.

It seemed to help bring some ease to her mother. The tension left her brow, and she even managed a smile. When she was tucked in bed, Paige went to the kitchen to get a glass of water, the meds and a notepad. Although the therapist had stressed that in order to strengthen and regain verbal skills, they should avoid writing as a method of communication, just this once, it wouldn't hurt. They'd focus on speaking skills again the next day. Right now, her mother was sad and frustrated. She needed to tell her something.

After her mother swallowed her meds, Paige gave her the notepad and a pen.

"Here, Mom. Try to write what you want to say. I won't tell your doctor. I know we're kind of cheating, but…" She smiled and pulled a chair closer to the bed, waiting while her mother wrote.

Come home. Live here.

Paige read the words and then looked into her mother's eyes which once more welled with tears. "I'm staying here, Mom, for as long as you need me. Don't worry about that."

It wasn't a lie, but it also wasn't the whole truth. She had a career in Albany. Although after Aubree's and Noele's murders the passion she'd once felt for the job had waned. She wasn't sure if she could do it anymore, or if she even wanted to.

TWENTY THREE

Cory threw another piece of wood into the woodstove. Outside, the wind and rain lashed the walls of the wooden cabin and pelted a steady thrum on the metal roof. It was enough to drive a man to drink.

After an afternoon taunting the wildcats, he'd had to call it a draw when the rain started. He'd barely got the fallen branches cut into chunks before the skies had really opened up. Dinner consisted of beans and mac 'n cheese. Both the can of beans and box of mac 'n cheese had been covered in dust; but the pickings around the cabin were getting pretty slim.

This sucks. I can't stay here. The old man has put me here to die. He doesn't care. Just so long as his life doesn't go off the rails. Cory pictured his father's house, a mansion really, with all the comforts of money. Too bad the old prick wouldn't die. There was a fortune there, and he was the only heir.

His brow furrowed with second thoughts. But how could he claim any of that with the police looking for him? Maybe that fancy lawyer could defend him again. She was smart. If anyone could get him off, it would be her. Grilling Noele, she'd made his ex look like a crazy liar.

Should he chance it? Count on her saving his ass?

A picture of the lawyer defending him before a judge and jury played in his mind like an episode of *Law and Order*. He lost himself to the movie in his head, the smart lawyer praising him as a concerned father who'd fled in shock and grief when he discovered the bodies of his only child and wife.

A pain shot through his bowels making him jump, jerking him out of the fantasy. Another searing bolt gripped his lower stomach.

The baked beans. The can was so old it was probably bad or something!

Shit!

He grimaced. *That was it exactly it.*

A bead of sweat glistened on his forehead while his intestines gurgled in knots. He'd have to go out in the rain, the dark, and that damned storm to use the outhouse. When the most intense cramp, yet, struck he leapt to his feet and grabbed his jacket. He'd be lucky if he got there in time. These were his only pants!

The door banged shut behind him and he almost slipped in the muck before he fished his penlight out to light the way. The outhouse was ten feet away, the entrance like an open mouth with the door hanging askew. Rain plastered his hair to his forehead and rolled coldly down the back of his neck, but he didn't even notice. The pain in his gut was white hot, searing through him. He stepped into the narrow hut and almost dropped the penlight into the pit in his haste to peel his pants down. He sighed a deep breath of relief sitting there.

But it was far from over when another cramp punched through his lower body. He panted, trying to catch his breath. He shivered from the cold creeping up his back. His hands shook when he floundered around for toilet paper. God almighty, he was weak as a kitten. This was definitely food poisoning.

The pain continued. What the hell? There was nothing left in him after sitting there for what felt like ten minutes.

A snarling howl, the cry like a banshee pierced his ears. Oh no! It was that lynx, and it was right beside the outhouse! He stretched forward and grabbed the handle of the door, yanking it shut.

Immediately the door shuddered. The sound of claws ripping at the wood, and another howling snarl followed. But that snarl had come from behind the outhouse. It was the two of them, back for revenge!

His face tightened. That wasn't the way that wildcats were supposed to act. Cats hate storms and getting wet. They should be hunkered under some rock overhang or something. What the hell was with these two?

With his heart hammering fast, his fingers fumbled in the pocket of his jacket. Damn! He'd taken that knife out and left it on the table. His cell phone was inside the cabin too! He was stuck out here in this smelly box, his bowels turned to water while those two cats stalked him.

"Get lost! Go away, you stupid cats!" He yelled as loud as he could, but the only answer was another screeching snarl.

A thud on the door was hard enough to shake the plywood structure. He felt it in his knees and feet. He waited for another, barely breathing. The pain in his guts was forgotten in the rippling shot of fear going through him. What if they managed to knock the outhouse over? That had to be the two of them that had leapt at the door.

CATS DON'T DO THAT!

They claw. They swipe. They even bite, but they don't act like linebackers tackling a wooden structure!

What the hell was with these two? They weren't acting right.

Rabies? Rabies can make an animal do crazy things. They had to be rabid. That had to be it.

He could wait them out. Like he had a choice?

The loudest snarl and scream yet was followed by a thud on the roof. Cory shone the penlight up to the rippled green plastic where four dark paws splayed. Oh my God. The roof wasn't even metal or wood. That hard plastic was *old.* It could crack from the weight and then what? He'd have a lap full of snarling teeth and razor claws.

He watched in horror as the cat burrowed and tore at the plastic, the scratching sound was loud, even drowning out the rain and wind.

It was just a matter of time before it fell through. Cory scrambled to his feet yanking his pants up and zipping them. If that monster came through, by hell he wasn't going to be caught with his pants down.

The building teetered to the side when the cat pounced to the ground. Cory threw his weight to the tilted floor slamming it back into place.

He crouched there, watching the roof for any sign of the cat. It was the most vulnerable part of the small structure. A steady drip of rain caught him in the eye and he jerked back. The roof had cracked! That damned cat had broken it! If it jumped up there again, it was bound to come through.

But there was no sound of the cats outside. Not even a rustle of leaves or footsteps. Only the rain pattering down and the whine of the wind through the trees.

Maybe they'd given up. If he didn't hear them again in ten minutes or so, he'd make a run for it, back to the safety and warmth of the cabin. He could do it.

One thing was for sure. If he made it back to the cabin, he was going to call his father. There had to be some place else to hide out that wasn't infested with rabid animals, or food that was poison.

'The old prick is trying to kill me.' His eyes narrowed at the thought. His lips curled in a grim smile as he pictured smashing a tire iron into the old man's skull. He could take the car and be in another state in no time.

TWENTY FOUR

The next day when Paige got back from grocery shopping and visiting the electronics store to buy her mother a new tablet, it was close to noon. Karen had stayed with her mother all morning but had a dental appointment early afternoon. They were like ships passing in the night when Paige came into the house.

She helped Karen with her coat. "Have dinner with us tonight. My specialty, lasagna and salad. Thanks for helping with Mom, this morning."

Karen patted her cheek gently. "You don't have to thank me. I love both of you. I'll bring dessert. That is if my mouth isn't still frozen from the dentist."

When she opened the door, she looked back at Paige. "You've got company!"

Paige edged by her. Sure enough Melanie's red Ferrari was tucked in behind the Honda and she was just getting out. She carried a basket of fruit wrapped in cellophane, her smile tentative seeing Karen. In the sheepskin jacket, jeans and sneakers, she was more like the Melanie Paige remembered.

"Well if it isn't Melanie Walker! I haven't seen you in years." Karen gushed over Melanie who broke into a grin.

"Karen Stearns. It's nice to see you." She leaned past Karen handing the basket of fruit to Paige.

"I hope you'll stay, so I get a chance to see you later, but for now I'm off to the dentist." Karen fluttered her fingers and then left the two young women.

"Good timing. I just got here myself from shopping." Paige closed the door when Melanie stepped inside. "Mom's in the kitchen. She was happy to hear you'd be visiting."

"Wouldn't miss it." Melanie winked and then slipped her jacket off to hang it on a hook.

Paige followed Melanie into the kitchen and set the basket of fruit on the table next to her mother.

"Cheryl! It's been too long. I had to come over to see you after I heard. But, I must say you're looking pretty good." Melanie patted the woman's hand and took a seat across from her.

Paige watched her mother's eyes widen watching Melanie. "What'd I tell you, Mom? It's hard to believe this is the same girl I used to hang around with." She smiled at her friend. "Thanks for the fruit, Mel. That was kind."

Melanie leaned closer to her mother, "I hope you like the fruit, Cheryl."

Her mother's mouth opened and closed a few times trying to speak. Seeing the frustration in her eyes, Paige jumped in. "Her speech was affected by the stroke, Mel. But I know she appreciates the gift. Look, I have to put these groceries away, but after that, you're staying for lunch, right?"

Melanie smiled and started to get up from the table. "Absolutely. Do you need help with that or—"

"No. Just relax. Visit with my mom. I'm sure she'd love to hear what's going on in your life since you left Madison."

Melanie took a deep breath. "It's been such a long time, where to start? Oh my God, I can't believe that it's been years since I left work at the library here. You were away at state college while I was learning library science at CalTec. That was another life."

Paige nodded at the memory. "A lifetime ago, huh?"

Nodding back, Melanie then turned to Cheryl. "I remember when we were little. You made the best brownies in the world, by the way. You always were so patient, especially when I slept over, talking and giggling late into the night. You must have felt like a zombie at work the next day."

Paige glanced over to see her mother smiling at Mel. "Those were crazy Friday nights all right."

Melanie continued. "I hope if I ever have kids I'll have that level of understanding."

Cheryl nodded with a smile.

Melanie continued. "For now, I'm doing a lot of traveling. I inherited a pile of money, so I'm seeing the world."

She looked over at Melanie when something else from the day before popped into her mind. "So what about this Seth you mentioned yesterday? Is it serious?"

Melanie's face lit up again. "Seth Peterson. Remember him from high school? He was a senior while we were only freshmen, so if you don't remember him that's understandable."

Paige's mouth had drifted open as Melanie spoke. "Seth Peterson? Of course I remember Seth Peterson! He was the star quarterback, smokin' hot! Everyone knew who Seth Peterson was." As odd as it was for "Mealy Mel"—her nickname in high school— to be with the high school jock, something else occurred to her. "Did you start going out before or after you became rich?"

"Jeeze Paige! *Before!* We dated occasionally, but there was always something special between us after I came back from college." She got up and plugged the kettle in to make tea. Her voice became a soft whisper. "He stuck with me through those tough times, okay?"

"Tough times?"

Melanie glanced over to Cheryl before urging Paige to step into the hallway. When they were out of Cheryl's earshot, she whispered, "Yeah, hard times. Look, besides the exorcism I told you about, I was in a mental ward, and he visited every damn day."

Paige's mouth dropped open. "A mental ward?"

Melanie nodded. "For a *month*. I was sent there right after that thing that happened with my friends." She leaned into Paige, keeping her voice low. "When they couldn't do anything for me, I was put up at a convent for another month."

"That's where they did the exorcisms?"

Melanie nodded. "Seth could only visit one afternoon a week then." She let out a sigh. "That man…" Shaking her head, she added, "He didn't even know about the money my friend Dara left me."

"Does he now?"

"Oh yeah. I had to tell him. He was worried how my insurance would pay for all this. He said we should get married and I get on his health plan." She waggled her eyebrows. "He's a fireman, you know."

Paige giggled. "That sounds *hot*!"

Melanie chuckled at the pun and rested her hand on Paige's arm. "He's good to me. He won't leave his job and become a 'kept man' no matter how much I nag. She cocked an eyebrow at Paige. "This is kind of weird," she added, keeping her voice down.

"What do you mean?"

"C'mon. One minute I'm bragging about my love life with a buff fireman at the same time I'm recounting my experience in demonic possession."

Who nodded. "Yeah. Weird."

"I'm okay, now, Paige." She glanced around the kitchen taking in the room. "Maybe all of that was meant to be so I could be here." She shrugged. "I mean, who else do you know you can tell *your* crazy story to, huh?"

"You sure you're up for this, Mel?"

"Never better."

Paige nodded. "I believe you. "You went through a tough time, Mel. I'm glad you're better." Taking Mel's arm, they stepped back into the kitchen.

Cheryl was trying to get up from the table. Paige asked, "You need help, Mom? Do you need to go to the bathroom?"

Cheryl shook her head 'no'. "Do you want to take a nap?" Cheryl nodded in reply. "Okay!" Paige replied with a forced smile. "Nap time for you, young lady!" Seeing her mother nod and smile sheepishly, Paige took her by the arm and helped navigate her from the room.

***

A short time later, Paige sat at the kitchen table downloading the app which the speech therapist had recommended. The tablet was pretty easy to set up, and her mother had loved how light it was.

Melanie stepped over from the sink where she just finished doing the dishes from lunch. "You think your mom's asleep by now? I could go through that chest while you're getting her tablet programmed."

"Hang on. I'll check." Paige got up and tiptoed down the hall to her mother's bedroom. When she opened the door she saw her mother laying on her side, fast asleep. She went back into the kitchen. "She's out like a light," she said, her mouth in a frown.

"Goody! Now we can snoop!" Melanie replied.

Paige replied with a shrug. "I guess so."

"What's up with you? You've never snooped on your mom? Ever?" When Paige shook her head, Melanie scoffed. "Not snooping on your parents? Ever?" She giggled and put a hand on Paige. "I got to tell you; *that's* weird. Everybody snoops in their parents' bedroom!"

"Not me." Seeing the disbelief on Melanie's face, she added, "Mom made me promise—a really serious promise, when I was a little kid." She looked to the side, recalling the memory. "She made me promise on my love for her that I'd never go into that chest."

"Why?"

Paige looked back. "I don't know. She wouldn't tell me."

Melanie snorted. "Well, that promise stuck, huh? Here you are, thirty years old and you *still* got the willies about snooping in there." She laughed lightly. "I'd go nuts with curiosity!"

Paige just shrugged. "It was just me and Mom, you know? She never made a big deal about it, and I just let it go, I guess." She looked over Melanie's shoulder to the sewing room "Until now." Going through the sea chest had to be done. But that didn't mean she had to like it.

Melanie noticed the apprehension in her face. "Paige. We agreed to do this." She grasped her friend's shoulders. "It's bigger now than a promise you made when you were a kid. We're trying to help a little girl!"

"A little girl who's *dead*."

"A little girl who's still suffering!"

Melanie held her friend's gaze. Finally Paige nodded and said, "I guess so." Her lips pressed together.

Melanie gave her a shake. "And it's not just her, Paige! I had that dream *again* last night. Except that this time I was there when she died! I saw her face when she was being strangled!" Melanie shuddered. "That poor child fought for her life…and lost." She let go of Paige and jabbed at her own chest with her thumb. "I'm being haunted by Aubree now! I'm going to end up back in the looney bin if this doesn't stop!"

Paige dropped back into her seat at the table. Poor little Aubree had died, her killer still on the loose. She was being haunted by the child, and now Melanie was caught up in this too.

"You're right, Mel. This is bigger than the promise I made." She looked up at her friend. "But we can't let my mom find out. Not now, in her condition, you know?"

Melanie nodded. "I understand."

Wait. Paige peered at Melanie. "You've been through some crazy stuff yourself. Are *you* able to handle all this?"

"Sure."

"Really? You'd told me you were possessed. You said you were in a mental ward. Then something about being in a convent and exorcisms? What the hell happened? You're sure you're okay, now?"

Melanie managed a small smile, "Absolutely. After the psychotherapy, and exorcisms —"

Paige shook her head staring at Melanie. "A demon... I can't even fathom that. My God, what you went through!"

Melanie laid her hand on Paige's. "If you're worried that I might still be under some kind of evil influence, don't. A couple of guys showed up that weekend and I'm glad they did. Well, Adam... He's a psychic. We kept in touch. He gave me a clean bill of health, spirit-wise."

"I believe you." Paige snorted. "After what's been going on in my life."

"Yeah, either we're both batshit crazy, or…"

The silence hung between them.

"It's definitely the 'or,' Mel," Paige finally said.

"Yeah. It is." Melanie stood. "Let's get to the bottom of this."

As Melanie rose, Paige grabbed her arm, "But be really quiet. Mom can't know we did this. It would really put her recovery at risk."

TWENTY FIVE

Paige stood outside the spare-room door keeping watch that her mother didn't come out. She shifted weight to her other leg and flinched when the floorboard let out a groan. Shit! How much more time did Melanie *need*? She'd been in there for almost ten minutes!

The spare-room door opened, and Melanie tiptoed out with the flat black box in her hand. Mouthing, "Got it." She flicked the light switch and closed the door softly.

Paige followed her friend into the kitchen. She couldn't deny the excitement and curiosity, but there was also that sinking hollow in her gut that she was about to tread all over her mother's privacy.

Melanie started peeling the rubber band off the box, but Paige stopped her. "No. Not here. Karen could be back any minute, or Mom might wake up. Put it in your bag."

There were tons of room in the oversized leather slouch that passed as Melanie's purse. "What did you find out?" Paige couldn't keep the question from jumping off her lips.

Melanie looked over at her after slipping the box into the bag. She sat down and leaned closer to Paige. "I think I found the connection. There's a bunch of newspaper clippings. I mean really old stuff. But they're from a paper in Poughkeepsie, of all places!"

"What? We don't know anyone in Poughkeepsie. What kind of clippings? What's the connection? I don't get it." Paige took a seat next to Mel.

Melanie's eyes were wide, and she gripped Paige's arm tight. "Michael Smith! There's an announcement of some couple getting married. Then there was another clipping where his picture was. It was a Christmas ad boasting of how well Michael Smith's real estate firm was doing and thanking his clients."

Paige felt all the air leave her chest. "Michael Smith. It's got to be some relative of Cory Smith. Why would Mom keep clippings about that guy though?"

Melanie's brow furrowed. "I wondered that myself. But the last name isn't a coincidence. There's a connection to Cory. Why else would the strange things, like the chest opening, the light in the room always coming on, be happening?"

Paige's gaze drifted to Melanie's handbag. "It was funny. I forgot to tell you, but when Mom and I were looking at pictures on my laptop last night, Aubree's picture suddenly appeared on the screen. Right out of the blue."

"*That* is weird."

Paige looked over at Melanie. "The strange part was how upset my mother got. I know she's sensitive and all, but her reaction was over the top, even for her. She was really upset."

"She must have read the news report. It was plastered there for days."

Paige nodded. "And she's kept clippings of a guy who is somehow connected to Cory."

The words were hardly out of her mouth before the answer punched into her gut. "Oh my God. Could *he* be my father?" Horror filled her chest. If Michael Smith was her father and related to Cory, then Aubree... She might be a cousin or...even her niece? The muscles in her chest became a vise making it hard to breathe.

Cory was her half brother? That was too horrible to even

contemplate.

"Paige! Stop. I know what you're thinking, but you can't know anything for sure! Snap out of it, Paige!"

"Snap out of what? What's going on?"

Paige and Melanie jerked back seeing Karen in the doorway. Neither one of them had heard her come in. The older woman's gaze flitted between the two of them. Paige's face flushed feeling like she'd been caught cheating on an exam. Melanie looked down at the table.

"What are you two doing? Where's Cheryl?"

After the burning shame, another emotion claimed Paige, making her deliberately rise to face her godmother. "You know about Michael Smith. He's my father, isn't he? When Aubree and her mother were murdered, Mom knew the connection to him. That's why she had the stroke."

Karen's eyes had grown wider and wider as Paige spoke. Her mouth snapped shut, and she stepped into the kitchen. In a hissed whisper, she said, "You don't know that! Where on earth would you get that idea? I know this murder had upset you Paige, but—"

Keeping her voice down, Paige faced Karen down. "It's true! We have the evidence! It was right there in Mom's chest, hidden away!"

As if to add salt to the wound, Melanie plucked the black cardboard box from her bag and held it up.

Karen's eyes were wide staring at the box. She sank down into a chair, her hand at her chest. For a moment Paige worried that she might follow the same path as her mother. When Karen collected herself enough to speak, her voice was defeated. "You shouldn't have found that. Your mother... She never wanted you to find out."

Paige sank down, kneeling in front of Karen. She took the older woman's hand in hers. "Why? I asked her again and again who my father was. She would never tell me. I just wanted to know. I wasn't going to try to include him in my life. Nothing or no one would ever take Mom's place. I just wanted to know who he was."

Karen looked down at Paige. "Cheryl had her reasons. She wanted to shield you from him. He's not a nice man, Paige."

Paige sank back on her heels staring at Karen. After all these years to finally stumble upon her father's identity, only to find out that the reason he was kept from her was because he wasn't "nice"? It was surreal.

But his connection to Cory jolted her back to reality.

This was worse than anything she could ever imagine. Could he also be Cory's father? Oh God. And this man's blood ran through her veins as well. She staggered to a seat at the kitchen table.

Melanie crossed the room to the sink, muttering, "Jack Daniels would be better, but water will have to do."

All the while Paige sat still as a statue, completely dazed. Her world had tilted off its axis. After drinking half the glass that Melanie handed to her, Paige scooped the small bracelet from her pocket. Tears filled her eyes as she gazed at it.

Aubree's MedicAlert. Her niece's? A niece she would never get to know— to hold, to sing to, and read to.

Melanie stood between Karen and Paige. She stroked each of their shoulders gently. "This is between the three of us. Cheryl will never know that Paige and I have uncovered her secret. That's the priority here. We tend to the living. But..."

Karen looked up at Melanie. "But what? What more can you do that hasn't already been done?"

"We get justice for this poor little girl and her mother." Melanie looked down at Paige, "You aren't anything like this man or Cory Smith. Michael Smith may be your biological father, but trust me, he was just a sperm donor."

Karen looked over at Paige. "She's right. You are your mother's child through and through. She's a good woman."

But none of it made sense. Paige shook her head gazing at Karen. "How? How did she ever get mixed up with a guy you say is so bad? I've seen pictures of her when she was younger. She was a total knockout. She probably could have had any guy she wanted. Why *him*?"

Footsteps from the bedroom interrupted their

conversation. Paige took a deep breath. "I think Mom's up now. I'll go in and help her."

Karen clutched at Paige's arm before she had a chance to leave. "I'll tell you everything. Tomorrow when your mother is in her therapy session. We need to talk."

Paige nodded and then left the room. When she entered the bedroom, her mother was pulling the coverlet over the bed, tidying up. She couldn't help but see her mother differently now. She looked past the weight that her mother had put on to see the young woman who had been with this mystery man. Paige still couldn't picture him, although she sure as hell was going to scour those clippings.

Her mom managed a smile and stepped over to Paige, planting a soft kiss on her cheek. She held her mother's arm as they walked back out to the kitchen.

Melanie had left, but Karen was busying herself making tea as if nothing was amiss.

TWENTY SIX

Later that evening, Paige read the text message that beeped on her phone.

"Where are you? I'm at the Crown and Pint but you aren't. WTF?"

Paige's thumbs flew typing her response.

"Sorry. I'm on my way now."

She looked at Karen and her mother sitting side by side on the sofa in the living room. It had taken longer than she'd anticipated getting Mom and Karen familiar with the speech therapy app. Now they were like kids with a new Game Boy, both of them grinning each time her mother was able to say the name of an object that appeared on the screen. As the therapist had said, "Baby steps at first."

"I won't be long, Mom. Just a drink with Melanie and I'll be back."

It was Karen who answered, "Take your time. Your mom and I will be fine. But don't drive if you've had more than one, okay?"

"No problem. I'm going to walk anyway." Paige grabbed

her coat and headed out the door.

Ten minutes later she entered the small bar where Melanie was. This time she'd taken a booth in the corner where they could have more privacy going over the contents of the box. Melanie had a drink waiting for her. She was smart enough to order a double Jack Daniels.

"Hi." Paige shrugged her leather jacket off and continued talking as she took a seat. "It's kind of sad to see Mom struggle to find the words for everyday stuff. But I think that program is going to help."

"Yeah. That's gotta be frustrating for her too." Melanie put the box on the table. "Ready?"

Paige lifted her glass and took a long sip. "Now I am." She pulled the box from Melanie's fingers and took a deep breath.

The first clipping showed a picture of a smiling blonde woman in a graduation cap. She was attractive yet there was a vacuous "Barbie doll" plasticity in her eyes. This was the woman who had actually married her father.

Next to that was a photo of a dark-haired man, in his twenties. Paige examined his face closely. The photo had been torn and half of his face was missing but what showed in his one eye and half mouth looked as solemn as a judge.

He wasn't classically handsome, but there was something about him that held her gaze. She searched his eye looking for some resemblance to her own. But there was too little to go on. She forced herself to read farther down the page.

"Mr. and Mrs. Robert Gallway are happy to announce the engagement of their daughter Lorraine May to Michael George…"

The groom's last name, like half of his face, was missing from the clipping.

She scanned farther,

"The happy couple's wedding will be held June 25, 1983 at the Church of the First…"

Again the church's full name was gone. Paige's brow tightened. Her mother had saved this announcement but hadn't been too careful in the way she'd ripped it from the newspaper. It probably showed more of her mental state that she hadn't clipped it with scissors.

She set the clipping aside and examined the next one. Her forehead knotted. This was the ad for his real estate company. Like Melanie had said, it was not so much an ad as a boasting testimonial of how well their firm had done that year listing the sales team under a cheesy Christmas banner. The words were smudged but the owner's name stood out—Michael Smith.

Could this guy in the Santa hat, beaming a fake smile *really* be her father? While his mouth was smiling for the camera, his eyes just looked dead. She couldn't place it, but they looked familiar.

Cory's eyes.

Melanie touched her wrist. "You okay?"

"I think so." She sighed, dropping the clippings back into the box. "At least now I have an idea what he looks like." Her eyes narrowed. The date of the wedding announcement was 1983. Almost a year to the day after her own birthday.

She looked over at Melanie. "If he knocked up Mom, he sure didn't waste time in finding someone new."

"How old is Cory? Do you think that couple could be his parents? Does it fit, age-wise?"

She knew Cory's age to be late twenties. It was possible. Definitely not a shotgun wedding though. "But if he's Cory's father then the police would have questioned him. I mean, Cory just vanishes into thin air? They'd turn over any stone that could lead to finding him."

Melanie's eyes narrowed. "Michael Smith is connected to Aubree. We know that. Why else would you have been directed to that sea chest? We need to pay Michael Smith a visit."

Paige pulled back from the table, staring at Melanie. "Go to Poughkeepsie? How... I mean, what can we say to him? 'Hi. I think you're my dad and by the way is Cory any relation to you?'" She could feel her neck muscles grow tighter at the thought of actually meeting him.

"No. Not like that." Melanie stared into her drink for a few moments. “He’s in real estate. Why couldn’t we pretend I’m looking to buy a house? You can be my attorney. You don’t even have to give him your real name. We’ll chat with him, and see what we can find out.”

Paige knew that this was destined to happen. Much as she dreaded the thought, there was no other way. “It could work. But it’s almost a three-hour drive each way. I’ll have to tell Mom that I’m needed at work for something, and see if Karen can look after her.”

“I know this is gonna be tough on you, Paige, but he’s practically the only lead we have in tracking down Cory. I’ll set everything up. Hell, I’ll even drive.”

“No way! Sure, you make the phone calls, but we rent a car. Something plain in case we have to tail him. Your flashy car would stand out like a sore thumb. And I’ll drive.”

Her gut was a tight knot of barbed wire. She was actually going to meet her father.

TWENTY SEVEN

The next day, after dropping her mother off at the speech therapist's clinic, Paige and Karen sat across the table from each other at a coffee shop nearby.

Karen's hands clasped together on the tabletop. The jittery twirling of her thumbs showed how nervous she was talking to Paige. After the waitress had served their coffee and left, she began in a low voice. "I never wanted to do this, Paige, but since you found some of it out yourself, you need to know the whole story."

Paige nodded. "Yes. It's time I knew." She leaned closer, and her hand rested on Karen's. "I promise I'll never let on to Mom."

Karen's eyebrows bobbed higher for a moment and sighed. "At least not until she's better." She paused for a few beats, staring out the window next to her. "You know your mother left home as soon as she legally could, right?"

Paige knew that much but not much more about what had happened in her mother's younger years. "Yes. I gather she wasn't close to her mother."

"Your mother was close to her *father* though. When he was killed in a car accident, everything changed. Your grandmother remarried and had two children right away. Three years after becoming a widow, she was remarried with two babies." Karen's eyes darkened. "It became clear to your mother by the time she was twelve that there was no room for her in this new family."

"You're kidding."

"No I'm not." Karen's eyes got misty. They kept 'forgetting' her birthday; that started when she turned twelve. When she graduated from high school, they couldn't go because her parents chose *that week* to take her half siblings to Disney World!" She looked at the two women. "Cheryl was an afterthought in her own home."

Paige's forehead knotted listening to Karen speak. What a miserable way to grow up. And considering how her mother had sacrificed, done without, to give her own daughter everything she could, it seemed doubly cruel.

"Well, your mother left home as soon as she could, and never went back. She moved to another city." She stared at Paige, and when she said the next word, it was like she spat out a bad taste. "Poughkeepsie. She got a job as a receptionist at a real estate company."

"Michael Smith's company."

Karen nodded. "He was just starting out, and the outfit only had a couple salespeople. Cheryl was naïve. She fell for Michael Smith's charm. She became pregnant with you."

"But you said he was a bad man."

"Oh, he was. She didn't really discover that until the night she was going to tell him she was pregnant. She said she'd seen the odd thing: losing his temper over silly things, bullying waiters, but what she saw that night really opened her eyes."

Paige pictured the man from the photo. She could almost see the cheesy grin hiding something dark underneath. Like Cory.

"He took her out to dinner, and when he was walking her home some panhandler approached them, begging for money to get something to eat. Cheryl said the kid was only sixteen or so, and old ragged clothes covering all ninety-eight pounds of him. Rather than ignore the kid, Michael berated him, telling him to eat shit and die. The kid turned away but told Michael he was a son of a bitch."

"Sounds about right."

"Yes, but when the kid turned away, Michael went after him. He beat the crap out of him, brutalized him till his face was hamburger. It was like he was possessed or something. Cheryl said there was rage, but something else too." Karen's eyes narrowed. "She said it looked like he enjoyed doing it."

Paige took a deep breath. "How did he get away with that? Was there no one there to stop it? Even Mom?"

"Your mother begged him to stop. He backhanded her away. Even the kid was begging him to stop! But he just kept on."

"Sounds like he's a mean drunk."

"That's the thing that really frightened your mother! He was stone-cold sober!"

"What?"

"Yes. He hardly drank at all. But on that street he beat that kid almost to death! It happened on a side street. All the stores were closed, and there wasn't anyone else around. It scared your mother so bad that she ran. When she got home, she packed a bag and left. She never wanted him to know about you." Karen sat back and looked at Paige.

"Yet she kept newspaper clippings about him. Why? Did she still love him?"

Karen's eyes sparked. "She was scared to death, Paige! Even though his firm was small he had lots more money than she did. He was also extremely jealous. If a man so much as looked too long at Cheryl, he would lose it. He'd staked his claim on her. His behavior kept getting worse until that night when he actually lost control. She had to get away from him especially since she was carrying his kid. She didn't want him anywhere *near* you."

Paige sank lower in the seat. All these years she'd resented her mother keeping her father's identity from her. But she'd done that out of fear. Just like Noele had feared Cory.

"Oh my God." She scooped Aubree's MedicAlert bracelet from the pocket of her jeans and held it tight. It had become a talisman, connecting her to Aubree. She stared at it. "I could have been Aubrey." She stroked the surface of the medallion.

There was a bond of blood between her and that child.

TWENTY EIGHT

While Paige heard the tale of her father from karen, Cory faced a whole other set of problems.

After trying numerous times to reach his father on the phone and getting only voice mail, he gave up. If he was to survive there was no way he could count on the old man. Still weak as a kitten, he shivered all through the long night. The fire had burned out, and there was nothing left to eat. His ankle looked even worse too, all swollen and red, pus oozing from the bites.

There was no way around it. He had to get out of there.

Arming himself with the table leg, he stepped outside and scanned the forest for any sign of the lynx pair. After the night he'd spent, shivering in the cold, his ankle throbbing while his gut felt like someone had taken a tire iron to him, he'd welcome seeing those cats. The table leg wasn't metal but it still could do a heap of damage.

The sky in the distance was heavy with gray clouds. The wind curled an icy hand over the back of his neck. He pulled the sweatshirt hoodie up covering his head. Each step across the uneven ground jarred his ankle, and he found himself using the table leg as a cane. When he rounded the bend the dirt road could be seen about fifty yards away.

Where the hell was he? It had been pitch black when the old bastard had dumped him there. Not to mention the fact that he'd been forced to stay huddled in the back seat. Which way should he go? It wasn't like there was any traffic. Who would come out to the back country at this time of year?

He gazed at the sky to see where the sun was hiding behind the bank of clouds. It was barely visible, just a faint blur hanging just above the tree line. That way was east—probably where he should head if he had any chance of getting back to civilization. His head hurt racking his brain for any clue trying to figure out how far till he hit a real road. If he could manage to get there, maybe he could flag down some car to get a lift.

His hand scraped over his face, rubbing the stubble on his cheeks. It was a start of a beard but nothing close enough to hide his identity. The old man should have given him some hair dye to get rid of the blond hair. The police would be looking for a blond.

He peered at the forest once more, checking for any sign of the cats from hell. But the only sign of life was a squirrel leaping from a high branch and landing in the tree next to it, rustling the dead leaves still clinging there.

His stomach grumbled as he set out on the narrow lane. What he wouldn't give for a plate of bacon and eggs. He'd gone about a quarter of a mile when he heard a low rumble, not thunder, thank God. It definitely sounded like a car's engine. The pain in his ankle spiked when he picked up the pace, hurrying to get over the crest of the hill to see if he was right.

Wheezing and cursing under his breath at his father and that damned Noele, he finally made it to the edge of the road. In the distance was a dark gray sedan making its way slowly along. For a second he panicked, tempted to hide in the cover of the forest. But the pain in his foot and hunger held him there. If he didn't get back to civilization soon he was as good as dead. He had to chance it.

When the car was about thirty feet away he waved his arm over his head. He didn't have to fake the desperation in his eyes. He could just make out an old guy clutching the steering wheel while he stared at Cory.

"Hey! Help me. I'm hurt and lost." He tried to look friendly. He didn't want to completely scare the old coot seeing a guy in the middle of nowhere.

The car slowed and came to a stop beside him. Cory took a step closer watching the window lower a few inches and the guy stare at him.

"Thank you, Jesus, for sending me some help!" Cory looked to the sky and then flashed a smile at the old man. "I hate to trouble you, mister, but is it possible that you could give me a lift to the nearest medical clinic or hospital? I was bit by a wild animal, and—"

"Where's your car? How'd you get in here?"

Cory barked out a short laugh, but all the time his mind was working overtime. "My wife. She up and left, stranding me out here. We were staying in a cabin, kind of a second honeymoon thing, but…" He looked down, doing his best shame face. "We had a fight. I woke up this morning, and she was gone with the car, phone and everything."

"Oh yeah?" The old guy's gaze wandered from Cory's muddy sneakers, the filthy pants and then to the scruffy jacket with the hood hiding his hair. "Where you from?"

Cory felt a glimmer of hope at the man's question. This might be easier than he'd even hoped for. He took a step closer to the car door with his best sheepish grin. "Walden." There was no way he was going to give the guy the truth. Who knew if his face wasn't plastered on every news channel?

"Walden? You're a long way from home, kid." The man chuckled.

Kid? Just the way the old guy had said that made Cory see red. The dismissive tone and calling him "kid" just like his old man. His voice was flat when he asked, "You gonna help me or what? I could use a lift to the main road at least."

The guy's steely gaze was back, and the window started gliding higher. Cory leapt and grabbed the door handle, yanking it wide. He was on the old man in a heartbeat, giving a quick jab to the old man's throat before jerking him up and out of the car. The old man clutched his windpipe, on his back beside the rear fender. The shock on his face was quickly replaced by fear as he scrambled with his hands and legs to get away.

"You should have just given me a lift you old geezer. Why'd you have to be a dick?" Cory grabbed the chair leg which had fallen to the side when he attacked the man. He stepped over and swung it up and over his head, bringing it down with a sickening thud on the old man's mottled temple. The old man cried out and tried to shelter his head with his arms, but Cory wasn't done with him...not by a long shot.

Again and again he clubbed the man's head and body, grinning as blood and tissue flew from the man's head. "Stupid! Stupid!" Each crack of the chair leg was punctuated by Cory's words and spit. It felt good...no...*way* better than good. It was *epic* serving justice to that old bastard. The nerve of him giving him the third degree and then trying to leave.

The chair leg fell from his hand as he bent gasping for air. The old man's face was a mass of red and his eyes were vacant staring at the sky. Only the car's engine gently idling, sending up a soft glimmer of exhaust broke the stillness.

When Cory straightened, after catching his breath, he stepped over to the old man and grabbed his hand. He was surprisingly light. He dragged the body into the thick undergrowth of trees. Cory's fingers reached into the man's pockets, and he plucked out a brown leather wallet. There were a couple twenties in there but not much else. He pocketed the money and then threw the wallet as far into the forest as he could.

A downed branch off to the side would help conceal the body. After tossing the chair leg into the forest on the other side of the road, he got into the car. Already the warm air from the heater made him feel better.

He had a car and enough money to get gas and a bite to eat at a drive-through. After that, he'd deal with his father. Plus, that was where the real money was. Enough to get him far, far away from New York State.

TWENTY NINE

That night, after the dinner dishes were cleaned up, Paige pulled out her phone to call Melanie. It rang only a few times before Melanie picked up, firing a question..

"Hey. How did today go?"

Paige sank into the kitchen chair, "Okay, I guess. How about you? Did you...you know?"

Melanie chirped excitedly, "Yeah, I called Michael Smith's realty office. I insisted on speaking to him, since I'm rich and only deal with the head honchos." She chuckled, "I can be a real bitch when I need to be."

Paige smiled for the first time that day. "No more Mealy Mel, huh?"

"That girl is way, waaay in the past, Paige."

"Good." She looked down at the floor and her voice lowered. Mom and Karen were ensconced in the next room watching 'The Price Is Right'. "So? How'd he sound?" She bit her lip as she waited for Melanie to tell her. About her father.

"Like any other blowhard salesman. He's got exclusive listings of luxury homes where the owners are seriously motivated to sell. He tried to pawn me off on one of his sales agents. I had to do a little flirting to get him to commit to working with me. I can still taste the vomit up in my throat from that, but I did it."

Paige sat straighter, staring wide-eyed at nothing. "*What?* You got this set up already?" Her heart beat faster in her chest.

"Of course. We're going to meet with him tomorrow afternoon. He probably ran a credit check on me as soon as the call ended. It's all set up. I told him I have many dealings in the Big Apple but I don't want to live there. The two hour train into the city works well for me. After some on-line noodling around, I was able to describe Michael Smith's house and neighborhood down to the letter. That's what I told him I was looking for."

Paige blinked a few times and her jaw which had slowly gaped open snapped shut. "Tomorrow? Oh my God." Despite the fact that this was the plan, the fact of it actually about to happen made her jittery.

"I've booked the rental car. I'll be around to pick you up at eleven tomorrow morning. Wear something lawyerly. Think you can pull that off?" Melanie laughed.

"Smart ass." She rose to her feet and wandered over to the counter to avoid being heard, "I'll I'll tell Mom that I'm needed to sign off on something at the office, but that I'll be back in the evening. Home care is supposed to visit her anyway, so between that and Karen, she'll be fine." She took a deep breath, trying to quiet nerves which were taut as piano wires. "Thanks Mel."

"Don't thank me yet. We've still got to come up with a plan that will lead us to Cory."

"We'll figure it out on the way there."

***

After Paige broke the news that she was needed at the office the next day, she purposely avoided her mother. The woman would see right through the lie if given half a chance. Karen knew what was really going to happen and made it clear she thought it was a bad idea by shaking her head 'No' behind

Cheryl's back. When her mother's head was turned away, Paige shot Karen a dark look that quieted her objections.

Paige took her time in the bathroom, showering and getting ready for bed. She held the bracelet in her hand before she left the room. It might have just been her imagination but she felt a sense of peace settle into her body holding it. She was on the right track in the quest to find Aubree's killer. The details would come to her later.

When she left the bathroom, Karen was just closing her mother's bedroom door.

The older woman whispered, "Your mom said she was tired, so I helped her get ready for bed. I'm not sure though…" She crooked a finger, beckoning Paige to follow.

Once they were in the kitchen, she spoke, "I think she suspects something. Of course she didn't say anything but she kept looking over her shoulder, expecting you to come out to join us. She seemed agitated."

Paige felt the weight of guilt settle in her chest. This was exactly what she had hoped to avoid. Of course her mother was suspicious. She'd never been able to tell even a white lie to her without the woman knowing. "It's only for a day, Karen. Once I see Michael Smith I'll know if he can lead us to Cory."

Karen glared at her but her words showed more concern than anger, "How do you know that? He's not stupid, Paige. Even if he knows where Cory is, he's not going to give that up. You should let the police handle this. I hate you going anywhere near that man."

"I can handle this. He'll slip up if he's hiding Cory. And when he does, I'll be there to catch him."

Seeing the firm set of worry in Karen's face, Paige added, "This is just an interview to see what I can find out. Believe me, I'll call the authorities if I get an inkling of where Cory is. I'll be careful, I promise."

Karen gripped Paige's arm and leaned in, "You better be. I think he's a dangerous man. Don't turn your back on him for an instant."

Paige smiled, "Well, Melanie will be with me."

Karen shook her head, "I'm not sure if that makes me feel any better about this. She sure has changed since the last time I laid eyes on her." Karen sighed and made her way to the front entrance. She took her coat from the hook and turned to Paige, "I'll be here at nine tomorrow morning. Good night." She opened the door and left.

Paige locked up and as she passed by her mother's room she paused. She should really go in to say goodnight. But she couldn't stand the thought of telling any more fibs to the woman who had done so much for her.

This would all be over soon. She would make it up to her mother after this thing ended.

For now, she had to finish this.

THIRTY

When Michael Smith woke the next morning, the first thought to invade his aching head was Cory. Had he been foolish to toss the burner phone connecting the two of them into the trash? Cory would surely have tried to contact him. Food had to be running out. Plus, it had sounded like the idiot had somehow hurt himself. His son must be getting desperate.

Maybe he should cancel his appointments and head out there to check on him. The last thing he needed was for the kid to somehow show up again, unannounced. But how could he get out to the cabin without attracting attention? There was that car that in all likelihood were cops staking out his home and office the last few days. No, he couldn't chance it.

He flipped the down comforter aside and pushed his feet into his slippers. Dry scrubbing the sleep from his eyes he plodded into the adjoining bathroom. He should never have helped the kid, never have gotten involved with any of it. When he looked in the mirror, the bloodshot eyes staring back at him told the tale of a restless night even after killing half a bottle of whisky. That was another thing the kid had screwed up. It was almost two years since he'd had a drink and for the last few nights he'd hit the bottle pretty hard. Hell. He had to, to get any kind of sleep at all.

Screw it. This would be over soon. The kid couldn't last out there and if he somehow made it out of the cabin, the cops were bound to pick him up. When they did he'd be free of Cory. Deny. Deny Deny. That was the motto he'd always lived by.

His mouth twitched with worry. But the kid had something on him! That stupid hooker! Cory said that he'd blab to the cops to cut a deal if he had to!

Wait a damn minute. There was absolutely zero evidence on him regarding that episode. He had never been questioned by the police over that matter… He nodded his head sharply when he realized that if the kid tried to pin that on him, he'd simply ask why the boy knew so much about that crime? The boy who's arrested for murder? He spoke aloud, trying on the tactic: "Maybe his wife and child weren't his first victims officer?" Yeah, that would probably work! If the kid tried to drag him down, he'd turn the tables on him so damn fast!

When he finished in the bathroom he wandered into the kitchen. Sunlight streamed in through the French doors, casting a glow on the granite countertops and aluminum appliances. He hit the button on the coffee maker and then took a seat at the island, booting up his laptop while he waited.

First the financial reports on the economy. His stocks were in good shape although oil still hadn't rebounded as much as was forecast. He flipped to local news but an alert caught his eyes. The body of a retired state trooper had been found on Pond Road in Levin? His eyes opened wider and he clicked the link to read more. Pond Road? Levin? Shit! The old lady's cabin was on that road.

His heart beat faster reading that when the man hadn't returned home by nightfall his wife had contacted the police. A search team with trained dogs had turned up the body a few hours later. The victim, Herbert Reid, had been driving an older Chrysler sedan. It was missing. The victim had been beaten to death and the assailants were believed to have stolen the vehicle.

Cory! It had to be him that killed the guy. Michael's fist clenched so hard his manicured fingernails bit into his palm. The kid had a car now. Two guesses where he was heading.

Michael got up and scuttled to the window, checking the fenced patio and sides of the backyard. But nothing was disturbed there, with the chairs still propped onto the table and the view of the lake below. That lake with the house sitting practically on the side of a cliff overlooking it had been why he'd bought the place. That sharp drop off the back of the deck exposed so damn much of the lake; it was really beautiful at sunset…

He gave his head a shake. He's thinking about views of the lake below when Cory could be here right now? He's losing it! Okay, the back of the house looks undisturbed, but what about the rest of the place?

His heart raced, his pulse thundering in his ears as he raced to the dining room window to check the side yard. Again, there was only the lawn bordered by stately blue spruce and birch trees. The living room window showed a view of his driveway, his Escalade tucked close to the flagstone walkway. As he passed the front door he thanked his lucky stars for the state of-the-art security system he'd installed years ago. Cory may be in the neighborhood, but there was no way he was getting inside the house without him knowing it.

He checked the other rooms, the office, the spare bedroom and even the family room at the back of the house. There was no sign of anyone or anything amiss in the lawn bordering the house.

Maybe he'd gotten lucky. He took a deep breath as he walked back to the kitchen to get his coffee. Maybe the kid had taken off and was across state lines by now. He could only hope.

One thing he was sure of, if Cory showed up at his house, he was calling the cops. The kid was going to go down for what he'd done, but he sure as hell wasn't taking Michael with him. He sipped his coffee, still on edge, staring out the window to the patio.

He could stay holed up there all day and see how this played out. It wouldn't be an entire lie to call in sick to work. His head throbbed from the Jack Daniels, and his chest felt so tight he wondered if he might have a heart attack. It would be all that damned nitwit's fault if he keeled over.

By the time he'd finished the coffee, his nerves felt less jangled. He could do this. Despite Cory still being out there, he couldn't deviate from his normal routine, not if he had any chance of looking innocent.

Shit! He *was* innocent! It hadn't been him who choked the life out of that little girl or her skanky mother. That was all on Cory!

But would they believe him when he said he had nothing to do with helping the kid get away?

Shit. The cabin. It could be traced back to his office. And then there was the little matter of how his son had gotten to a place that was probably not even on Google Earth.

"Screw it," he said aloud. "If they take him in alive, I'll lawyer up and play the concerned father." That was a good plan. Even so, he had to hope that if the little shit was hanging around out there that the cops would kill him in the arrest. Dead men don't tell tales.

In the meantime he had to avoid suspicion. That meant going in to work as if nothing happened. He didn't know about any murder up in Levin or where his son currently was. That was his story, and he'd stick to it like glue.

As for the day's schedule, it might work out perfectly. That rich woman was looking for a house, and coincidentally the Clarke's down the street was listed with his company. It was even vacant if she needed to move in right away.

He could show her that and keep an eye out for Cory at the same time. Hell! He'd even show her his own home if that's what it took. The house was too big now, and he'd been toying with the idea of buying a condo. It might really work out well after all.

He could do this. He was Michael Smith after all.

THIRTY ONE

The last thing I wanted to do was visit a mall today." Paige flung the car door open and scowled over at Melanie.

"You couldn't be my lawyer the way you were dressed! Sorry, but jeans and a leather jacket would not cut it. Furthermore, *I* paid for the new outfit. What are you complaining about?" Melanie rolled her eyes before yanking the seat belt across her lap.

Paige started the car and sat still for a moment. They had plenty of time before meeting with Michael Smith. It wasn't like the shopping excursion had cost them much time. It was nerves, plain and simple. Now that they were only ten minutes from meeting with him, she was wired tight. "Well, thanks, but I could have paid for them, you know. It's not like I don't have a good job. I mean I'm a lawyer for God's sake."

Melanie shot her a look. "Then how about *acting* like one, huh? Aren't you legal eagles supposed to be insufferably arrogant?" She slumped lower in her seat. "Look, I know this is hard on you. The whole situation is screwed up beyond words—meeting your father who is also that maniac's dad? Just let me do all the talking, okay?"

Paige eyed the rearview mirror before pulling out of the parking space. She had to admit the clothes were perfect even if a pant suit was something she tried to avoid normally. But the navy color and formfitted cut projected money and success. As far as letting Mel do the talking she was totally fine with that. She wanted to size the guy up first and foremost. "Have you thought about how you're going to get him talking about his family?"

"Of course. You just leave that to me. I'll have him spilling his guts. I'm not the police. People tend to open up to me. Not that I always want to hear their sad story. I have enough crap to deal with in my own life."

Paige glanced over at Melanie. After what she'd learned about Melanie's experience in the Catskills, she'd believe it. For a few more minutes they drove in silence, each mentally preparing for the interview with Michael Smith.

Up ahead was the small strip mall where the Smith Realty sign dominated high above the others. She flipped her turn signal on and pulled into a spot in front of the office, beside a black Escalade.

Melanie turned to her. "Ready?"

Paige nodded. "Let's go ramify 'em, Addy."

"Addy? Ramify? What's that supposed to mean?"

"Lame joke. Sorry." Paige got out of the car and reached into the back seat for her new satchel. Another touch that Melanie had insisted upon.

When they entered the office, Paige took in everything at a glance—the Berber carpet, leather chairs and sofas. The waiting area bordered on being a greenhouse with all the tropical plants.

A pretty brunette sitting behind a desk turned from her monitor to smile at them. Paige thought of her mother, how this was probably the same position her mother had filled when she worked there.

Melanie strode over to the counter, her wide-leg palazzo pants swaying while the ends of a silk scarf draped over her brocade jacket fluttered beside her. "I'm Melanie Walker. This is my attorney, Fran Lewalski. We have an appointment with Michael Smith."

Paige cringed at the name Melanie had assigned to her.

She'd even managed to print business cards with the horrid moniker on them.

"Of course." The woman rose to her feet rounding the corner of her desk to extend her hand. "I'm Marcie, Mr. Smith's assistant. He's expecting you." She nodded her head and then led the way to the office set near the front of the building.

Paige took a deep breath to quell her jitters. Damn! She was here for Aubree! The fact that this man was also her father was incidental. Wasn't it? She pictured a courtroom and the set of tight nerves that always preceded a hearing. Yet once the judge was seated she'd always settled into the groove, her mind cool and alert. This couldn't be any worse than that.

Yet when she laid eyes on him, her breath hitched in her throat. There he was. Sitting behind a desk, his olive-colored eyes a mirror of her own. But that was where the similarity ended. Even though he was six feet tall, he was portly, looking like he'd never set foot in a gym in his life. His hairline that had once been pronounced in the photos had receded at each side, the gray littering dark hair that was slicked straight back. She might have inherited his height but she was slender and fit.

"Miss Walker." Michael rose and shook Melanie's hand before glancing at Paige.

A waft of sickening sweet cologne hit her nostrils. If came off Michael Smith in waves. She'd dated a guy, Frank Gambotti, who'd worn that same cologne—Polo. It hadn't improved Frank's sex appeal, and on Michael it was truly revolting.

Paige looked away, breathing through her mouth as she gazed at the oak furnishings, the award and certification plaques adorning the wall. She barely heard Melanie's response as she forced her lunch back to where it belonged in her stomach.

"Oh. I hope you don't mind, but I brought my attorney and friend, Fran Lewalski. I'm hoping to finalize a purchase today and wanted her advice."

"Not at all!" Michael turned to peer at Paige, extending his hand. "Miss Lewalski. Pleased to meet you."

Paige stared at his hand for a quick beat before she shook it murmuring, "Nice to meet you, Mr. Smith." She glanced into his eyes before taking a seat next to Melanie.

Yes. The guy had something about him. A confidence and masculinity that she could understand her mother being attracted to. The smile that had blossomed on his face had been too quick though. Almost as quick as when it vanished before he turned away to go back to his seat.

"Would you like water or coffee?" Marcie's voice made Paige startle but Melanie smoothly answered.

"No. We stopped for lunch before we came in. We're fine. Thanks."

When Marcie shut the door softly behind her, Melanie once more was all sweetness and light. "Mr. Smith, I'm so glad you found the time to meet with us. I know how terribly busy you must be. But I always insist on dealing with the owner of any business. I mean, you know what you're doing, and I don't have time to waste."

"Absolutely. I completely understand—"

"I confess that I'm probably not as good as this as I should be. My ex-partner, Ross, used to look after all our living arrangements. That's why I wanted Fran here. She's like family to me." Melanie actually looked down in her best Princess Di pose. "Family is so important. Don't you think? Do you have family, Mr. Smith?"

Paige was torn between wanting Melanie to shut up and let the man talk or nausea from her blatant flirting.

Michael Smith glanced at Paige before answering Melanie. "I had a family. But like any modern marriage, it didn't last. My wife, or rather ex-wife, lives across the country now."

"How sad. Children? It's always so hard when children are involved. Tragic really." Melanie actually eased forward in her chair, a picture of concern.

"Well...yes. A son. I practically raised him single-handedly." For the first time, Michael looked away and his face became harder.

Paige tried to look away so as not to call attention to the fact that she was hanging on to every word. This was it! He admitted he had a son. It had to be Cory.

Melanie's hand rose, and she placed it on Michael's. "That's so sad. But he must be doing fine now! If he's anything like his father, he must be running some business or in politics perhaps? What's his name? Maybe I'll vote for him." She actually managed a giggle.

Michael cleared his throat. "Um...not exactly. But you said you were pressed for time. Perhaps we should get down to business. Based on what you outlined to Marcie, I have a few different properties that might fit your needs." He opened a file folder and slid a photo of a large ranch bungalow across the desk. "I printed these for you." He turned slightly and with a click of his mouse brought a larger view of the red brick home onto the screen.

Melanie pretended to examine the photo. Her mouth became a moue. "But the neighborhood. Is it exclusive? Gated? Where do you live, Michael?"

Paige slid the spec sheet toward her, trying not to gag on Melanie's honeyed tone. They already knew where Michael lived. Where was Mel going with this?

Michael slid a smile across his face. "I'm in Estoria. It's a quiet neighborhood on a bluff at the outskirts of the city. Gorgeous view of the lake. But there's no need for that degree of security, not in Poughkeepsie. No, you'll find gated communities more in Florida than here. It's part of the reason I stay here."

"Well, that sounds lovely! A view of the lake, you say? That's a bonus, isn't it, Fran?" Melanie turned to Paige and smiled.

"Yes. Are there homes for sale in your neighborhood, Mr. Smith? You've lived there all your life? Raised your son there?" Paige found it hard to meet Michael's gaze and looked away a few times. Shit, this was harder than she'd thought it was going to be! She had to get a grip. Her hand slipped into her pocket, and she clutched the bracelet once more. This was why she was here, damn it.

Melanie must have sensed her discomfort because she jumped in. "I think what Fran is alluding to is the fact that I want to have a family, children at some point, soon. If you raised your son there, it must be child friendly with schools nearby."

Michael nodded his head and rose to his feet. "Why don't we take a drive to a beautiful home in my neighborhood. It just came on the market and won't last long. I'll take you on a tour and show you the schools and parks nearby." He chuckled. "Gosh. I haven't actually shown properties in years. This is a walk down memory lane, but with two beautiful women beside me, I'm not complaining."

Paige peered at the credenza behind Michael's desk when Michael walked over to the closet to grab his overcoat. Pictures of scenery, award celebrations with dignitaries but no photos of his son or family. She'd been hoping for added confirmation, but Michael wasn't giving that up, not in his office memorabilia.

"Will we follow you or—"

"You'll ride with me, of course! I'd love the opportunity to get to know you better." The smile he flashed at Melanie was pure saccharin. "Especially as we may become neighbors."

Paige could feel his eyes boring into her back as they walked out of the office. Great. Confined in his vehicle breathing that vile stench. As if this wasn't bad enough.

"Mine's the Escalade." Making a show of being gentlemanly, he darted in front of Melanie to open the passenger door for her. He then opened the rear door, watching Paige with a small smile on his lips. "Fran. May I call you Fran?"

"Certainly, Michael." The name almost choked her but she got it out. There was nothing about this man, her father, that she liked. He was sleazy. But more importantly, he was probably Cory's father as well. Which meant Aubree was his granddaughter. His murdered granddaughter, yet here he was acting normal, just business as usual. Karen had said he wasn't a nice man.

That was a serious understatement.

***

Forty minutes later, after pointing out landmarks and schools, libraries and parks to Melanie, he flicked the turn signal on and entered a forested area. The road snaked through the wooded area as the SUV climbed higher and higher to the peak. Many times during the tour through the neighboring area his eyes had met hers in the rearview mirror. She had tried to keep her face impassive despite the distinct feeling that he was sizing her up.

Melanie continued her prattle, impervious to whatever silent communication was happening between Paige and Michael. Hell. Paige wasn't even sure what he was up to. She just knew it creeped her out. If not for the bracelet in her pocket, which she clutched hard, she might have asked him to stop the car so she could escape being near him.

But once they were at the crescent of the small mountain, where an outcropping of luxury mausoleum-like homes dominated with pristine manicured lawns and interlock stone driveways, Michael turned his attention to the neighborhood. He checked out the street and houses, his gaze furtive while his sales pitch petered out.

Melanie seemed to have tuned into the change in his attitude, looking back at Paige with question marks in her eyes. But she soon recovered and once more with a lilt in her voice, she asked, "Where is your home, Michael? I bet it's that massive ranch over there." She pointed, but her eyes skewered the man beside her.

He seemed to jolt from whatever fugue he was going through when he turned to her. "Yes. That's a pretty good guess. But it's this home here that I'd like to show you." He pulled into the driveway of a stone bungalow a few doors away from his own. Although with the large half acre lots it was still a ways off from his.

When he popped out of the car and was rounding it to

open their doors, Paige mumbled to Mel, "He's on edge. Ever since he entered this street he's been checking things out."

Melanie turned slightly to face her. "I caught that too. Keep an eye out, girl." And then the smile was back when the door opened, and Michael extended his hand to help her out.

"Why, this is lovely. It looks large enough, and the grounds are impeccable."

Michael opened Paige's door but he spoke to Melanie. "Most of us use a grounds keeping service. You won't see any of your neighbors cutting their lawns or shoveling snow. We're all too busy plus it's kind of a social norm here. That way, things are kept nice."

He led the way up the walkway and after consulting his phone, he keyed in the security numbers to disarm the alarm and open the door. He held it for them and explained. "There's no gate for security, but everyone in this area has an alarm system. We sleep better knowing it's there."

For the next thirty minutes Melanie and Paige followed him from room to room as he expounded on the unique but luxurious features of the home. When Michael wasn't looking at them, Paige and Melanie exchanged looks, shaking their heads. Both of them knew where they really wanted to go with this.

As they were leaving the house Melanie paused watching Michael lock up. "You know, it's a lovely house, but I was really hoping for a view of the lake. What I could see was just a sliver of a peek through the evergreens. Yet you have a full vista from your house. Is that right?" She sidled closer to him and giggled. "You wouldn't consider selling me your house, would you? I'd give you whatever you asked."

Paige had to turn away to stifle the gag. She never would have guessed that Melanie would be this good at flirting and manipulation. The little wallflower who wouldn't say "boo" had blossomed into a first-rate Venus Flytrap.

But would Michael Smith be dumb enough to fall into that trap?

THIRTY TWO

A day earlier...

Cory was twenty minutes into the drive with the heat cranked all the way up in the old geezer's car. His teeth chattered, and his arms twitched clutching the steering wheel.

"Damn it!" He fumbled with the knob trying to crank more heat out, then sat back listening to the warm air whoosh from the dashboard. But still he shivered while a cold sweat beaded on his forehead. Even his vision was blurry and he had to shake his head to clear it. It was hard to navigate on the winding back roads, even though he'd left the cow path long ago.

His foot, on the accelerator, was numb and there was a dull pressure on his ankle. Looking down at it, he could see the cuff of his pants pressed tight on his flesh. With the way that ankle was swelling up, he needed to get antiseptic or drugs to stop the infection soon.

There were only fields broken by outcroppings of forest in the rolling hills that he drove by. He hadn't passed a house in at least five minutes, let alone get to a town with a clinic or pharmacy.

When he rounded a slow bend in the road, a sign on the shoulder caught his eye: *Town of Gardner 2 Miles'.*

There had to be a drugstore there where he could get fixed up. A clinic would be better, but he'd need money and ID for that. The town wasn't far. He could do this, and with some food and aspirin in his belly he'd be able to get the second wind he needed to get to his father's house.

A few minutes later, he came up to another sign that said, *'Welcome To Gardner'.*

As he was passing by the sign a child stepped out from behind it. He gasped, his eyes wide with shock. Oh my God! Aubree?

She turned her head as the car rolled past, her face impassive. He was mesmerized as her hand rose, finger pointing straight at him.

The blaring honk of an oncoming car caused him to jerk. He swerved the wheel just in time to avoid a head-on collision. His heart hammering, he looked in the rearview mirror, but there was only the sign and the gravel shoulder of the road to be seen. What the hell? He blinked hard trying to get a glimpse of her.

He yanked the car to the shoulder, threw it into park and spun around to the back window. She had been wearing that same damn red plaid coat!

Where'd she go? She'd been there only a second before. But how?

Aubree was dead.

Oh my God. His hands shook, but this time it wasn't from the cold. He was sicker than he'd thought—hallucinating that he'd seen his daughter. His foot eased up from the gas pedal, and he took a deep breath. He had to get control or he was gonna have an accident. Forget the damned infection in his foot! He'd be dead in a car wreck if he didn't get a grip.

A sign posting a lower speed limit along with a few houses looked promising. He'd soon be in some shithole town where he could get some relief. With any luck the police wouldn't be looking for this car. The old geezer probably wouldn't be missed for a day or so.

Soon, houses bordered the road, and he could see a traffic light up ahead, along with a few neon signs above small stores. His stomach grumbled as he passed a Chinese restaurant, the aroma of food flitting through the car vents. He smiled when he saw the Rite Aide sign. A drugstore that also would have food and other things he needed. He flicked the turn signal on and pulled into the small parking lot, stopping next to a red truck.

When he got out of the car he staggered a bit, forgetting in his eagerness that his foot was numb and swollen. A woman walking her dog on the sidewalk looked over at him and hurried by. Shit. He must be a sight. The same clothes for four days, with mud and blood smeared on his pants from the raccoons and that old geezer. He took a deep breath, grimacing inwardly at the pain but trying to look as normal as he could.

When he went into the store, a young woman at the cash looked up from where she was reading a magazine. He smiled and nodded to her and hurried down the aisle to where the pharmacy was. He grabbed a bottle of aspirin, antiseptic ointment and bandages before crossing over to the hair-care aisle. After looking around to see if anyone was near he slipped a package of men's hair coloring into his pocket.

As he approached the cash, he grabbed a bottle of water from the cooler as well as a large bag of potato chips. Not the most nourishing food but it would do for now.

The girl set her magazine aside and forced a smile, revealing a line of braces on her teeth. Her eyes behind the thick glasses were huge peering at him. "Find everything you need?" She looked down and started scanning his items.

"Yeah." He spotted a rack of eyeglasses at the next register. "Hang on." He looked for a a pair with thick dark frames and tried them on. The lenses were pretty weak because his vision only blurred slightly. "I'll take these too."

"That'll be twenty-one, sixty-four."

He slapped the twenties down and waited as she gave him

the change. A few minutes later he was back in the car wolfing down the aspirin with the water. A look in the mirror showed a trace of blood on his chin. He'd take care of that once he'd cleaned the wound on his ankle with the ointment.

Wincing, he twisted in the seat to raise his leg and set his foot down on the seat beside him. He had to tug the cuff of his pants higher revealing the red mottled puff of his ankle. The puncture marks were black and oozed a clear liquid when he pressed the ointment there. A red-hot searing pain shot through his leg when he rubbed it into the wound.

He sucked in a long breath through gritted teeth and then sat there for a long while. The noise of a deep-throated engine startled him, and his eyes shot open. It was the red truck next to him. He hadn't even heard the guy open the door and get in.

He'd actually fallen asleep? Oh my God. But he had to admit he felt a little better. Better enough to find a thrift store and get some other clothes. Maybe even find a diner where he could grab a coffee and start work on his hair in the men's room. He tore the bag of chips open and then started the car. One thing was certain. He couldn't just sit there like a lame duck waiting to be caught. He had to get to his father's house to get some money and another set of wheels.

***

It was almost 10 p.m. when Cory arrived in his old neighborhood in Poughkeepsie. He cruised by his father's house slowly, noting the Escalade in the driveway and some of the lights still blazing inside. The old bastard was home and still awake.

Tempting as it was to knock on the door and get inside where it was warm, there was no way he could chance it. The old man hadn't returned with supplies and hadn't even bothered answering all the calls for help he'd made from the cabin. It was obvious that he wanted nothing more to do with him. The old prick was more worried about his own skin than helping his own flesh and blood.

And forget trying to break in. The place was like Fort

Knox. The cops would be there in a New York minute to lock him up.

No. The only way he'd get help from the old man was to jump him when he came out for work the next morning. He'd use the element of surprise along with a tire iron to get what he needed.

It would mean spending the night in the car but he could do that. At least he had warmer clothes and a blanket thanks to the Family Thrift store. He drove out of the exclusive subdivision making his way down the winding road until he saw what he was looking for. If you didn't know the area, the narrow road leading into the wooded area would be easy to miss. The only people to use it were the contractors who kept the steep and twisting road cleared in the winter. Their shed full of salt and sand was tucked in under a stand of trees around a bend in the lane. No one would be going down that lane anytime soon.

Cory parked on the far side of the shed and cut the engine. He downed a few more aspirin and then stretched out as best he could on the back seat. The fleece blanket provided a little warmth but his ankle still throbbed like a jackhammer.

Twenty minutes later he was sound asleep, worn out by the pain and his body fighting the infection.

THIRTY THREE

Michael felt unsettled from the first moment he laid eyes on the lawyer. He'd never met the woman yet there was something familiar, something that put him on edge. All the while that the rich bitch prattled on about family and wanting a secure neighborhood to raise a child, he'd kept sneaking glances at the lawyer.

The honey-blonde hair pulled back revealing a smooth ivory forehead and dark arched eyebrows...eyes that tilted ever so slightly in the outer corners, always eluding a direct meeting of his gaze straight on, like she was nervous or something. And she was tall for a woman, almost five ten in low-heeled pumps.

Of course she was attractive; they both were! But whereas Melanie with the heavily made-up blue eyes and high cheekbones had a flashy prettiness, the lawyer's beauty was timeless. She'd be attractive at fifty or even seventy. And she moved with the smooth grace of an athlete.

It was fortunate that he'd done this job all his life. He could go through the motions, rattling off statistics, dropping names during funny, humblebrag anecdotes while his mind worked on other things—like who the hell was this Fran Lewalski, and how did he know her?

He turned to punch in the security code, setting the lock on the house he'd thought would be a perfect fit for the rich millennial, when it hit him. Cheryl Evans. This Fran Lewalski was almost a dead ringer for Cheryl. Except for her height.

Melanie's voice brought him back to the here and now.

He glanced over at her when she sidled closer and giggled "You wouldn't consider selling me your house, would you? I'd give you whatever you asked."

Normally, he'd be all over that. Hell, she'd been practically flirting with him since they'd met, and her offer—well he wasn't blind. But he couldn't help staring at Fran who had turned away, her profile confirming the resemblances to Cheryl and his son as she looked up the street at his house.

"Well? I told you I came here to buy a house. Will you show me yours?" Melanie slipped her hand along his arm.

The words that flowed from his mouth were on autopilot. "Of course. I mean everything is for sale. It's just a matter of agreeing on price." He flashed a warm smile at her and then directed his attention to Fran. "As Melanie's attorney, what do you think, Fran?"

The woman had hardly said boo since she'd been with them. It was silly, but he wanted to engage her in the conversation. She wasn't Cheryl, but she sure as hell could be her.

Oh my God. The smile dropped from his face before he completed the thought. Cheryl's daughter? But that couldn't be. Her last name…

When Fran turned and smiled at Melanie, it hit him like a punch to his gut. That *was* Cheryl's smile.

"I think you should show your house to my client. Melanie is like a dog with a bone. When she wants something she usually gets it. It could prove to be mutually beneficial, Michael."

He nodded and then walked over to the car, holding the door for Melanie but his gaze riveted on Fran. "It's a great home to raise children, Fran. Are you married? Have a family?" The odds of this woman being any relation to Cheryl were astronomical but still something deep inside made him probe.

Melanie flitted by him and took her seat. When he held the door for Fran she seemed to falter just a little before answering. "No husband or kids. I'm too busy with my career. Especially with this crazy lady as a client." She slipped by him, avoiding eye contact once more.

And *that* was disconcerting. Almost as odd as the color of her eyes. An olive shade? He knew that color. He looked in the mirror everyday at that same greenish brown.

As he rounded the car to take his place behind the steering wheel, his mind warped into overdrive. Cheryl had disappeared into thin air after that night. He'd let her leave in order to calm down after the incident with the young panhandler—the stupid loser. But when he'd knocked on her door the next day, she was gone. Vamoose. Pulled a total Houdini on him. He'd searched high and low for her. For weeks he'd torn up the state.

Was it possible that she'd been carrying his child? She'd been so excited that evening at dinner. They were going back to her place to spend the night. But all that had changed when that loser mutt had tried to beg money from him. He'd totally lost it!

It was far from the first time he threw someone a beating. But it was the first time he had a witness. He knew he shouldn't have, but by God he worked hard, and the guy showing up out of the blue like that had ruined what should have been a perfect night.

Shit! He'd even had the ring in his pocket, everything all set to propose to her. All he could think of was the homeless guy ruining everything.

When he settled behind the wheel and started it up, Melanie peered at him. "Are you all right, Michael? You look upset."

Her words had a sobering effect. This wasn't how he conducted himself. He'd learned to hide that side of his nature long ago. Unlike his asshole son.

He forced a tight smile. "Sorry. Guess I'm thinking of how my life would change if I sold you my house. Thinking of how much I'd miss this neighborhood. But nothing lasts forever, right?"

He pulled out of the driveway but noticed Melanie exchanging a look with Fran. As he navigated the short distance to his own driveway, he glanced in the rearview mirror, "Where do you practice law, Fran? Are you based in Madison like Melanie?"

He would have to be blind not to notice her eyes flash wide meeting his gaze in the mirror. She immediately looked away again, fiddling with her purse.

He knew that look. She was hiding something. He glanced over at Melanie. She'd checked out financially, but it had been odd how she'd insisted on only dealing with him. What were these two up to?

THIRTY FOUR

Earlier that same day, as Michael was finishing lunch at the deli before he met with Melanie, Cory was sound asleep in the gray sedan. He had climbed into the back seat so he could stretch out as much as possible.

His eyes flickered open at the sound of a pinecone from overhead thudded against the hood of the car. He groggily sat up and looked at his watch.

Shit it was almost noon? He had slept for more than fourteen hours? He shook his head to clear the cobwebs. Damn. There was no way his father would still be at the house. The old prick prided himself on being the first one in at the office every day, setting an example for his staff.

He leaned over to have a look at his ankle to see if the ointment had done its work. For sure the aspirin had helped, to a fault. Thanks to it he'd overslept and missed his chance at getting the jump on the old man. His ankle looked a little less swollen and the puncture wounds only showed a glaze of the ointment, no pus or anything oozing out. That had to be a good sign, right?

After sliding the cuff of his pant leg down, he reached for the bottle of water on the floor and finished it off. His stomach growled, reminding him that he hadn't had a decent meal in well over a day.

Maybe the guy who owned the car had some money, or even a candy bar in the glove box? Cory's old man had always kept a couple of packs of beef jerky in their car. "Just in case we ever got stranded," was what the bastard had said. Yeah, he'd make sure there was food in his car, but could give a damn about looking after his own son stranded out in the woods.

He reached over the seats in front and fiddled with the latch. It flopped open and his eyes widened. Not a damn thing to eat, but…

"Holy shit, a gun!" he said out loud. He pulled it from the compartment. Snuggled inside a leather holster was a revolver. He undid the snap and pulled it out. It was in good shape, no rust at all. It was small, just a little bigger than the palm of his hand. He pushed the sliding button on the side and the cylinder flopped out, showing five bullets. It was loaded.

He smiled. Great! Dad wasn't going to give him any static when he came calling for his money now! He closed the cylinder back into the frame with a solid click before scrambling over the seats into the front.

He started the car and turned the radio on to a local channel.

He blinked hard, stretching his eyebrows high as he listened. There was the usual inane banter between two wannabe comedians before they announced the news broadcast. He was about to change stations when he heard the broadcaster mention Pond Road in Levin.

Pond Road? He'd see a sign with that name. Driven on that very road. His hand shot out to turn the volume up while he stared hard at the radio.

"A roadside robbery took the life of a retired state trooper today. The body of Herbert Reid was discovered along the side of Pond Road last night. Mr. Reid, a thirty-five-year veteran of the state

police had been last seen driving his car, and the public is being asked to keep a lookout for a 2014 gray Chrysler 300, license plate GAP-453. The vehicle is believed to have been stolen by the person or persons responsible for Mr. Reid's death. If you see this vehicle, do not approach, but call 911."

Cory stopped breathing, his eyes darting to the wooded area and the narrow dirt road behind him. Shit! He'd been lucky to escape notice driving this car. There was no way he could chance it anymore, even driving the short distance to his father's house. Suddenly the car's refuge from the chilly weather outside felt like it had a bull's-eye painted on the side of it.

He scooped up the bottle of aspirin and ointment and shoved them deep into the pocket of the sports jacket. Grabbing the tan overcoat from where it had slipped onto the floor he opened the car door and stepped outside. He jammed the firearm into his pants, pulling his shirt over the butt.

He'd roamed these same woods lots of times when he was younger, so finding his way to his father's house would be easy. Even though taking the road would be faster and more direct, there was no way he'd chance walking on it. Not even an exercise junkie would undertake the steep road leading to the mountaintop community. He'd stick out like a sore thumb, especially with the incriminating car nearby.

It would take him almost an hour trekking through the forest, but he could follow the road for most of it while still being well hidden from sight. If he could make it to that glade of trees near his father's property he could hole up there waiting for the old man to get home from work.

The constant climb on uneven ground was playing havoc with this ankle. Even trying to favor it by keeping as much of his weight off it as possible, walking was hard when he had to navigate around fallen logs and outcroppings of rocks. Being weak with hunger and a slight fever wasn't helping either. But that would all be taken care of when he got home.

The road rounded a curve, and he was forced to venture out from the wooded area. The stand of trees was interrupted by a sheer wall of granite that would be impossible to climb. If he went around it going deeper into the forest it would add fifteen minutes to his walk. He decided to chance it, walking on the road for fifty feet or so. As he was about to leave the cover of trees he heard a car's engine.

He ducked back and watched the blacktop from behind a huge maple. The thrum of the engine became louder, and soon the nose of a black SUV showed at the crest of the road. As it got closer to where he was hiding he could make out a man and woman sitting in the front seats.

His eyes widened seeing the familiar face. His father? On his way home already and with a young woman? And then he noticed the second woman in the back seat. What the hell was the old man up to? The car rounded the bend and disappeared from sight.

Shit! He was going to miss his chance again of getting the jump on his old man. And what was even worse was the fact he wasn't alone.

His eyes narrowed as he hurried along the roadway exposing himself to whoever might also be driving by. He couldn't go back to the stolen car, and it looked like his chances of getting the jump on the old bastard weren't all that good either. But still. What choice did he have? Of all the times for his father to pick up some hookers and party hard! The stupid old pervert.

He was out of breath, and his ankle hurt like a bastard when he once more entered the cover of trees. It wasn't far now. He could see part of the Leary's house which marked the beginning of the neighborhood. Just another ten minutes or so and he'd be there. His heart hammered hard, and he had to swipe a bead of sweat from his brow despite the chill in the air.

When he came to the outskirts, peering at the row of ranch bungalows and split-level homes lining each side of the wide street, he jerked back seeing the dark SUV parked at the

Clarke's house. And then it hit him. The Smith Realty For Sale sign. His father was showing the Clarke's house to those two women. They had to be some kind of big-shot prospects for his father to be personally working with them.

He leaned against the thick pine trunk watching the house through the dense hanging branches. For a few moments the pulsing pain in his ankle was forgotten as he contemplated his next move. He could cross the street and take a chance that his father hadn't reset the lock when they'd entered the house. Maybe he could go inside and…

No. There were the two women plus his father. Plus he'd never been in that house before. Who knew what could happen? Best to wait it out.

He settled in, trying to make himself as comfortable as possible. His father would finish showing the house and then later that evening he'd go home by himself. The odds of overcoming the old man at that time would be better. He scooped the aspirin from his pocket and dry swallowed a few for good measure. He'd be waiting for a few more hours anyway.

For some reason Aubree's face flooded his mind's eye. He could have sworn that he'd seen her at the sign the day before. If she was up there in heaven she was probably having a good laugh watching him shivering, skulking around his old neighborhood like a thief.

His jaw muscles twitched. Well, by this time tomorrow he'd be far, far away. Maybe he'd even get as far as Florida and be basking in the sun on some beach. He'd have the last laugh then all right.

He straightened up when the door to the Clarke's house opened and a willowy blonde stepped out. He peered at the entrance and a second woman followed. He took a few steps from the tree, staring hard. The way she moved and her height was familiar.

No. It couldn't be. He squinted his eyes, still trudging closer, examining her face, the honey-blonde hair falling over the collar of her jacket, the lean athleticism of her body. Oh my God. It WAS her. His damn lawyer, Paige Wright! What the hell was *she* doing there?

He watched as they all got into the old man's SUV. He couldn't figure out what the hell the house showing had to do with anything. His ears starting ringing as he put two and two together.

His old man had abandoned him at that cottage. Now he's talking to his damn lawyer.

That old bastard. Dad was getting ready to turn him in! That had to be it!

THIRTY FIVE

Paige cleared her throat and held her head high, sitting straighter in the seat. Her heart thundered against her rib cage as she tried to compose herself. Something was definitely off with the way Michael was looking at her. She'd sensed him sizing her up in the office and then as they toured the house, but he'd really gotten peculiar in the last five minutes. His gaze seemed to go straight through her, watching her like a cat watches a mouse. Had he caught on that he was being played?

The phone in her satchel buzzed sending a slight vibration through her thigh. "Excuse me. I've got to take this." It was a brief reprieve from having to answer Michael's questions, thank goodness. But at the same time her gut clenched tight wondering if it was Karen, once more bringing bad news about her mother.

When she pulled it from her bag, she jerked back seeing what filled the small screen. Aubree's face!

The young girl's eyes were wide with fear staring back. It was exactly as she'd appeared in Paige's dream.

But what shot a jolt of fear up her spine was the timing! It had been days since she'd encountered any sort of communiqué from the little girl. Why now?

Melanie broke the silence that had descended like a shroud. "Is everything okay?"

"Ye...Yes. It's just a text message. Nothing important." Paige clicked the button turning the phone off before placing it back in her purse. She glanced in the mirror to see if Michael had noticed her shaking fingers or look of horror when she'd seen the child. But he was already easing out of the car.

When his door shut and they were alone Paige hissed a whisper at Melanie, "It was Aubree. Her face just showed up on my phone!"

Melanie's mouth fell open for a second before she exclaimed, "We're meant to be here! We're getting close now." And just like that her face transformed into a gushing smile when Michael opened her car door. She took his hand as she stepped out. "I can't wait to see your house. I've got a good vibe already."

Paige kept her gaze down as she arose from the car's back seat. She only hoped that Michael couldn't see how nervous she was. But a quick glance at him showed his gaze flitting over the homes and sidewalks nearby. If he'd noticed how alarmed she'd been a few seconds ago, he didn't show it.

"I'm not sure my house is big enough for your needs, Melanie. It's got a great view but there are only four bedrooms. I know you're a busy woman, and I don't want to waste your time." He stood there for a few moments as if deliberating on whether to sell.

Paige stole a glance at him. It could be a tactic intended to drive the price of his house higher, yanking it from Melanie's reach. But considering how he'd been questioning her and the looks, it was more like he wanted to get this over with. He didn't seem comfortable standing in his driveway, and his warm repartee had grown chilly in the last five minutes.

"It won't take long. Plus with the oversized lots Melanie could add on if she needed to." Paige barely managed a smile when she turned to Michael. "Money isn't a problem for Miss Walker. She'll know right away if this house is what she's looking for."

"Fine." Michael led the way to the front door, pausing to disarm the security system and locks."

All the while she followed him, Paige had her hand thrust deep in the pocket of her jacket, holding the small bracelet in her palm. If it were up to her, she'd bail on being anywhere near Michael Smith as soon as was humanly possible. The man was a sleazeball. But being there wasn't all about her. It was about finding Aubree's killer. There'd be something inside that house which would tie him to Cory. Seeing Aubree's face on her phone confirmed it. She had to do this for Aubree.

Just where they'd take this was unclear, but they had to keep going. Melanie reached over and squeezed her hand as they waited for Michael to unlock the door.

When the door opened, Michael stepped inside holding the door wide for them to enter. There was a hard set to his jaw when Paige went past him. The sight of him closing the door behind her increased the tension. He stared at her with an odd expression as he ushered them through the entranceway.

Melanie's voice trilled through the air. "Now *this* is a view! Why, you can see across the lake and almost to the end of it. This is fabulous."

Paige walked into the kitchen where Melanie stood. "Breathtaking view. And the kitchen looks like it was remodeled recently. All new appliances, I see." All the while that she pretended to admire the cabinets and granite countertops, she was searching for photos, any sign of Cory or Michael's granddaughter.

Michael walked over to the table and the full-length glass patio doors leading to an expansive deck. "In the summer, I often have my morning coffee out there. It's too cold right now to go out there but trust me, it's lovely. The back drops off for about thirty feet and the view is magnificent. "

"You're so high up here," Melanie cooed. "The house on the hill!"

He turned to Paige again, the smile dripping from his lips. "You look very familiar to me, young lady. Perhaps I knew your mother or aunt? What is your mother's name?"

Michael held Paige's eyes like a cobra about to strike. "Her name is Cheryl, isn't it?" he said. His voice was low and smooth, but glittered on the edge.

Paige's mouth dropped open.

"Isn't it!" he shouted.

She jumped at the ferocity in his voice as he strode across the room to stand in front of her.

"Hey!" Melanie said from the kitchen. "What the hell's the matter with you?"

"Shut up, you!" Michael's face was beet red as he waved his arm at Melanie. He turned back to Paige, his voice now soft. "And you..."

Dangerously soft words.

He lifted a hand and brushed it across Paige's face. "You have the shape of Cheryl's face, my dear…but you have my eyes."

Paige was still as a statue from Michael's explosion.

"What the hell are you doing here!" he shouted, spraying her face with spittle.

She stared up into the eyes of her father, terrified.

As scared as I was of MY father, Paige! Aubree's voice echoed in her mind. At that moment the MedicAlert bracelet in her pocket grew hot. She backed up a step from Michael and fished it out of her pocket.

"Like father, like son," she said, looking down at it in her hand. Her eyes blazed with derision when she stared at him. "I just learned that you're my father. I also learned there's not much difference between you and Cory. You're both violent and out of control."

"What the hell do you know about my son!"

Her heart dropped. "I am a lawyer. And Cory was my client. I'm the one who…" Her voice faltered. "It's my fault he was able to kill Aubree."

Michael's face twisted in confusion. "You're Cory's lawyer."

"Yes! Where is he?"

"What makes you think I have any idea?"

Melanie had come out of the kitchen into the dining room. She stood beside Paige. "Let's get out of here, Paige," she said. "This isn't working."

The three of them jumped at the sound of the front door slamming and footsteps running up the hallway toward them.

THIRTY SIX

Hi, Dad!" Cory said, rounding the doorframe. "Hi Paige!" he added. "I wonder just what the hell you two are up to?" The ice-blue eyes staring out of his scruffy face were dead and cold. He'd changed his hair color, a cheap dye job that showed smudges on the skin next to his hairline. He looked like hell.

"Cory!" Michael said, turning. "This woman's your sister!"

"Oh really?" Cory's voice had dropped to the same dangerous purr Michael had a moment ago. "Is that so? From which whore?" He was a little unsteady on his feet and leaned on the doorjamb. He fumbled at his waist.

And pulled out the gun.

"What the hell!" Melanie said, backing up. She grabbed at Paige's arm.

Cory stepped from the doorway. "I know what you two are up to…" He gestured at Michael. "You, you bastard, left me in that cabin to freeze to death or die of starvation. Then you changed your mind, and decided to turn me in!" He gestured at Paige. "You brought in my lawyer so you could get your story straight, and you were gonna send the cops to pick me up!"

"Cory, you're crazy!" Michael said. He stepped over to his

son. "You miserable punk! Give me that damn gun before someone gets—"

BOOM!

The sound of the gun firing inside the house was an explosion. Michael staggered back, his hand to his throat, blood gurgling over his fingers in a river.

"Someone just did get hurt, DAD!" Cory stepped forward and put the pistol to his father's chest and pulled the trigger again. The sound of the second shot was muffled by the contact with the man's chest, and Michael fell to the floor dead.

Cory's eyes glazed over as he stood over the body, his face sallow with wonder. "Wasn't all that hard… Killed my wife… Killed my kid… Killed my father… Gonna go out west, find the bitch, and kill my mother… But first…" He lifted his head and looked over at Paige and Melanie who were frozen against the wall in shock. "My sister!" He raised the pistol.

The MedicAlert was red hot in Paige's hand. A keening screeching voice screamed in her head, *Throw it at him, Paige!*

Her hand snapped out and flung it into Cory's face. Paige saw it spark in midair before landing on his cheek like a branding iron.

"AAAAAAA!" Cory screamed, clawing at his face.

"Get him!" Melanie cried out. The two women rushed at him and knocked him to the ground.

Paige fell on his back. She whipped her arm around his throat, pulling back on his neck. "Get the gun!" she screamed at Melanie.

Like an enraged cat, Cory rolled over, bashing Paige to the floor. He scrabbled on top of her, sitting on her chest.

"Daughter!" He grabbed her by the neck and lifting it, pounded her head into the floor. "Father!" He did it again. "Mother! And sister! I'll kill you all!" Each word was punctuated by the sound of Paige's head striking the carpeted dining room floor. She saw the MedicAlert bracelet embedded in his cheek, the flesh around it smoking. "I'll kill all of you!"

BOOM!

The force of the bullet knocked him completely off her. Dazed, Paige turned to see Melanie holding the weapon in both hands. She looked back at Cory to see him scrabbling his hand at the top of his chest where the bullet hit him.

"Don't you move!" Melanie said.

Cory didn't hesitate for a second. He scrambled to his feet, and Melanie shot at him again, missing this time.

"I'll be back!" he yelled at the top of his lungs. Covering his face, he crashed through the patio doors onto the deck. Like an Olympic runner, he vaulted the railing at the back and dropped over the edge screaming as he fell. A shriek that ended abruptly.

Paige staggered to her feet, clutching Melanie's arm. They both ran through the broken glass to the railing of the deck and looked down.

Twenty feet below them Cory's corpse was splayed out on the side of the hill. Even from the distance, they could see from the sickening twisted angle of his head his neck was broken.

THIRTY SEVEN

Six months later.

"This really pisses me off," Melanie said, draining their now traditional Jack Daniels double. "Your richer than *me*!"

They were celebrating the surrogate court's final decision to award Michael's estate to Paige.

"What can I say?" Paige replied. "I'm his only living blood relative, and Mom had all the paperwork." She sighed. "She didn't want me to find my original birth certificate that named him as my father. That's why she kept the trunk locked." Taking a pull from her own drink, she added, "She told me that she held on to it because one day it might come in handy."

Melanie nodded. "The birth certificate was the clincher along with"—she paused— "the blood tests and DNA from the autopsy."

Paige blanched at the word. For the last six months she'd gotten pretty good at putting that behind her. Actually, she and Melanie worked hard at putting it behind *them*. From that horrible afternoon, they had been spending a lot of time together. For the first week they had both slept in the same room at her mother's home. They were afraid that they'd have nightmares, but none came.

They slept like babies, and considering what they had been through, it was surprising.

That week-long slumber party reconnected their friendship to a depth neither of them expected, and both of them treasured. They went through the police reports together, which was a breeze. Law enforcement was perfectly happy accepting their story—all the physical evidence supported it, and to be able to close out the murderous spree of Cory's without so much as a trial was a blessing as far as they were concerned.

"I didn't realize he was so loaded," Melanie said. She leaned across the table. "You don't feel guilty taking any of it, do you?"

"Nope. I *am* going to split it three ways. A third to my mom. A third to Cory's mother, and the rest to me."

"Still makes you stinking rich." Melanie shook her head. "Your father—"

"Don't use that term. He was a sperm donor, that's all. He had nothing to do with me and meeting him almost got me killed!"

Melanie waved her hand. "Yeah, yeah. Well, *Michael* was some kind of wheeler-dealer. Apartment buildings, vacant lands, a *ton* of cash we know about. The son of a gun was a real hustler."

Paige shrugged.

"Doesn't make you feel weird at all?"

She shook her head. "The weird factor of that is nothing compared to Aubree, hon." She took a breath. "I can't get over how I've never heard from her again."

Melanie snorted. "Me too. The kid moved on."

"Yeah…but it's like she was never here outside of what we both know… They never found that MedicAlert bracelet."

It was Melanie's turn to shrug. "Not to mention there wasn't a mark on Cory's face from it." She toyed with her glass. "We spent hours looking for it from where he had fallen. It's gone, Paige, and I think that's fair. That bracelet was connected to Aubree. Aubree's moved on, and she's taken it with her, I guess."

The two women sat looking at each other in silence.

"Still weird!" they said in unison and laughed. That aspect of them saying the same thing at the same time had been happening a lot. *She's the sister I never had,* each of them thought to themselves.

"Well," Paige said, "I'm glad this chapter in my life is over."

Melanie shook her head. "I'm not sure about that."

"What—you planning on going to law school or something? Come into practice with me?"

"No… It's something that's been on my mind since all this crap started."

"What are you talking about?"

Melanie swept her arm around her, gesturing in the air. "I don't know… It's just that…" She ran her hand through her hair before returning her eyes back to Paige. "Look—up until now, you ever had anything to do with the paranormal?"

"Nope."

"No séances or Ouija boards?" When Paige shook her head again, Melanie said, "That's my point. A year ago, I went through some hairy stuff with this kind of thing. Then I reconnect with you who's going through some crazy shit."

"You didn't reconnect, Mel. Aubree called you."

"That's my point! Why the hell me? I mean, we hadn't seen each other since high school!"

"We were friends."

"Yeah, but *why me*? I really didn't do much."

Paige burst out laughing. "Just saved my life!"

"Well, yeah, okay…but nothing 'ghosty' or stuff, right?"

Paige shrugged. Yeah, if there's one word to describe what was going on…weird surely works.

She lifted her glass for a toast. "To Aubree. Rest in Peace."

"To Aubree, may you stay wherever you are!"

They smiled and took a sip.

The End

Author's Note…

I *really* enjoyed bringing Melanie into this story. Actually, she appeared pretty much on her own as I was creating the first draft of this novel. I was merrily scribbling along and without any warning, her car appeared and she jumped out yelling at Paige.

Believe me, I was as surprised as you at her appearance, and I'm glad with the part she played in this novel.

Please feel free to leave an honest review if you're able. They help independent authors such as myself, yes; but more importantly, honest reviews from readers like you are a great help for other readers in making their buying choices.

As always, I'm deeply grateful for your readership.

Warmly,

Michelle Dorey

ABOUT MICHELLE DOREY

A multiple bestselling author, Michelle Dorey has written more than a dozen spine-chilling novels featuring ghosts, haunted houses and the supernatural.

A voracious reader of the masters like Stephen King and Dean Koontz, her debut novel was inspired by attending a Ghost Walk in the enigmatic city of Kingston, Ontario, Canada. Crawley House was inspired by a true tale of a family's nightmare, living in a Victorian era home.

"Expect the supernatural when the bedrock of a city is limestone. When this ancient rock is surrounded on three sides by water as my home town is... well, you have the perfect setting for eerie events—which of course is my cup of tea."

Wife and mother, Michelle is also a dog lover, human to Suki and Ruby. She loves them dearly, but for the last eight years on walks, they absolutely refuse to enter grounds of a beautiful historic cemetery near her home.

Michelle has written two complete series, The Hauntings Of Kingston and The Mystical Veil. She's currently at work on her latest, The Haunted Ones—set in upper New York State.

OTHER WORKS
BY
MICHELLE DOREY

THE HAUNTINGS OF KINGSTON SERIES

The city of Kingston is enigmatic; where the line between this world and the next becomes quite hazy. A ghostly series inspired by this historic and sometimes mysterious place. Each novel is a stand alone:

Crawley House
The Haunted Inn
The Ghosts Of Centre Street
The Haunting Of Larkspur Farm
The Ghosts Of Hanson House

THE MYSTICAL VEIL

Twenty four year old trust fund brat Keira Swanson finds out that her family has secrets. Secrets of the dead…

Legacy
Heritage
Forsaken
Ascendant

PARANORMAL SUSPENSE

The Haunted Ones

Ordinary people confront malevolent spirits in each of these eerie tales…

The Haunted Hideout
A Grave Conjuring
Haunted By The Succubus
The Haunted Gathering
The Haunted Reckoning
Graveyard Shift

SPECIAL BONUS:

The first two chapters of

GRAVEYARD SHIFT

Book 6 of The Haunted Ones

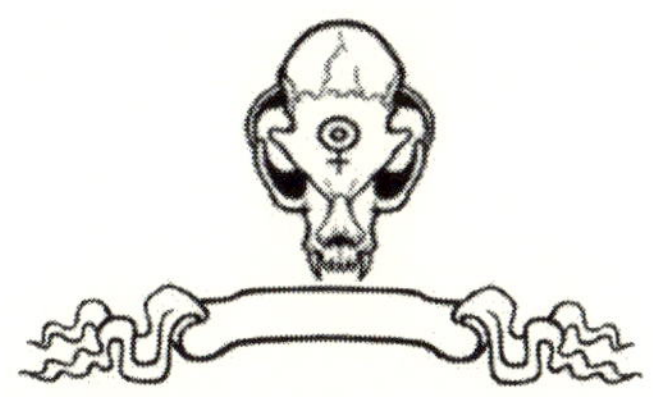

ABOUT GRAVEYARD SHIFT

Serenity Lodge is haunted. Don't ask the residents suffering dementia if that's true. Ask the nurses.

Amanda Ennis is the new nurse at Serenity Lodge nursing home. It's a dream job after years of the hectic pace in the emergency room of a large hospital. Better yet, she's on the short-list for an upcoming Supervisor position!

The only stumbling block to working there is the constant undermining from Linda Harper, a battle-axe nurse. They both want that Supervisor job. Linda believes her decades of experience entitles her to it.

Working with Linda was the only downside until the new resident, Carmel Turner, arrived.

Now, shadow people lurk in the hallways. Unseen hands play with the lights turning them on and off. Carmel, a psychic with stage-four dementia, claims she's even being attacked!

Amanda never believed in the supernatural until her own chilling encounters. When mysterious claw marks are slashed on Carmel, she can no longer deny their dire presence. Each new incident escalates the danger. But how can Amanda tell anyone? Ghosts? Spirits? If she so much as mentions this crazy stuff, not only will her promotion vanish, she'd lose her Nursing license!

All hell breaks loose on All Hallows Eve—that night when the barrier separating the afterlife is weakest.

No one is left unscathed. Not everyone is getting out of there alive.

GRAVEYARD SHIFT

MICHELLE DOREY

The Haunted Ones 6
Paranormal Suspense

ONE

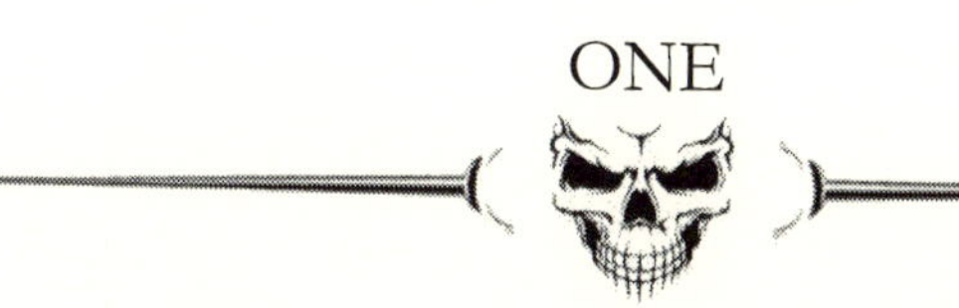

Help me! No! Get away! Leave me alone!"

Shrill screams pierced the slumber of the nursing home. Courtney jerked upright and peered at Amanda. "What the hell?"

Shrill screams pierced the quiet slumber of the nursing home. Courtney jerked upright and peered over at Amanda. "What the hell?"

"It's room 11 the new patient." Amanda vaulted to her feet and rounded the counter of the nursing station. Courtney's hurried footsteps were right behind her. Shrieks at the end of the corridor magnified to a keening wail.

What the hell was going on in there? Amanda bolted into the room, taking a deep breath as she flicked the light switch. A frantic old lady was clinging with one hand to the headboard of the bed, as her free arm waved wildly in the air behind her.

"No! Don't touch me!" The elderly woman's leg thrashed out, barely missing the pair of nurses.

Amanda ducked under the swinging arm and gripped the woman's shoulder. "Carmel! Easy. You're safe. You're having a bad dream."

"Help me! Get them off me!"

From the other side of the bed, Courtney reached out to grasp the old woman's hand, holding it in both of hers. "Hush. You're all right, Carmel. We're here. You must have had some crazy nightmare."

"Make them stop! Help meee!" The old lady's hysteria gave way to tears, her hunched shoulders wracked with sobs.

"What's wrong with her?" Jane Drogan, the room's other resident, was sitting up in her bed, her sheet bunched under her chin. Taking a deep breath, she plucked her glasses from the night stand next to her bed and gaped at Carmel.

Amanda ignored Jane and continued speaking to the distressed woman. "It's okay, Carmel. There's no one here, but us. You're safe."

Courtney stroked the old woman's arm, her voice softly soothing. "Let's get you settled, Carmel. Would you like something to drink? Water? Milk?"

Carmel jerked her hand away. She turned to Amanda. "Don't you see them? They're there! Cold, cold hands, pawing at my skin! It wasn't a dream." Her eyes glistened with tears. "This is a horrible place. Why am I even here?"

The plaintive whine in the older woman's voice tugged at Amanda's heart. To live such a long life and end up with hallucinations, reduced to hysterical tears, was beyond sad.

It wasn't all that different from the times she'd comforted her daughter, Kelly, when she was a toddler waking from a nightmare. What a cruel fact of life to revert to dependency, like a child, during your final days.

"Carmel, you're here because you need to be. Do you remember Dr. Stone? He admitted you for your own safety." Attempting to reassure the old woman, she added, "The first night in a strange place is usually difficult. But Serenity Lodge is a pretty nice place. You'll get used to it."

Jane squawked from the other bed. "It *was* a nice place. That was when you could get a decent night's sleep without someone screaming their fool head off, waking the entire country!" The gray-haired woman across the room punctuated her remark with a 'humph' as she settled under the covers.

Courtney threw a glaring look at Jane before she continued reading Carmel's chart. "The doctor has authorized a mild tranquilizer for you, Carmel. It will help you sleep."

"Give her the whole damned bottle."

"That's enough, Jane. Go to sleep." Amanda then turned to Carmel, repeating what Courtney had suggested. "First nights are hard, Carmel. Let us get you some water and a Lorazepam tablet. I'll stay with you until you go to sleep, if you want. How does that sound?"

Carmel swiped the tears from her cheeks and nodded. "Okay. But promise me you won't leave me alone." She slid lower on the bed while Amanda held the blanket high to tuck her in. "It was so real. There were three of them coming at me. Their eyes were black holes in their face!" Carmel's eyes widened. "But I knew they could still see me!" Her eyes darted from side to side as she chewed her lip. Looking back to Amanda, she said, "They were dead! But they weren't dead!" Her mouth worked open and closed in a silent scream. "You had a bad dream, Carmel." Courtney had returned from the hallway and now stood across from Amanda. She held out a glass of water and a small cardboard cup with a small blue pill. "Take this. Things will look better after a good night's sleep."

Amanda watched the older woman's hand quiver as she took the pill and water. She swallowed hard, tossing her head back to wash the medicine down.

Amanda glanced over at Courtney. "I'll stay with her."

Courtney sighed, "Four more hours 'til shift change. Now that I'm up, I might as well make the rounds before I go back to the station."

Amanda watched Courtney slip silently from the room. She knew exactly what Courtney was getting at. Staying awake during the twelve hour shift was extra hard when you were alone at the nursing station. At least when they were together they could chat and even share a laugh.

Amanda pulled the chair from against the wall and set it

next to Carmel's bed. The old lady's eyes shut and she snuggled deeper into the covers. Amanda stifled a yawn. Already, soft snores came from the bed across the room. Jane didn't have any trouble getting back to sleep.

Watching the old lady's chest rise and fall, Amanda took a deep breath. The relaxation of Carmel's muscles, and her mouth falling open, showed that the pill was already taking effect.

As she watched the older woman sleep, she couldn't help but wonder: what was Carmel's life story? Carmel was the first resident admitted without a family member to accompany her. On top of that, her patient file was the thinnest of any new admission; just the basic information, not even much medical history. But then... Carmel was also the first resident admitted by her attending physician, not a family member.

It was Dr. Stone who admitted her. He'd been working at Serenity Lodge for the last three months or so. She had yet to warm up to the middle-aged MD. His stand-offish, detached demeanor rubbed her the wrong way. It wasn't like he was an awkward genius. Hell, no; she had caught a bunch of errors on his part already. This guy had probably graduated at the bottom of his med school class.

Still watching the sleeping woman, Amanda stepped away from the bedside. She tugged her sweatshirt more tightly over her body, becoming aware of the chill in the room. The thermostat was regulated to drop a couple of degrees overnight to aid sleeping, but this was colder than normal. It was probably part of the 'efficiencies' the new owners of the home were promoting. Amanda snorted as she rubbed her hands over her arms to fight the chill. The 'efficiencies' were more like milking every drop of profit, cutting back wherever they could.

After watching the old lady sleep for a few more minutes, Amanda crept out of the room. She flicked the light in the bathroom off before opening the door and slipping out.

After a few steps she paused, turning her head, listening hard. Was that a noise coming from that room again? She could have sworn she heard a small thump. She stepped back and opened the door a crack to check. Both women were sound asleep in their beds, Jane snoring like a buzz saw.

It must be her imagination, brought on by bone-weary fatigue. Plus, four A.M. was the hardest part of a night shift. Once she got over that hump, getting meds ready for the morning and finishing her report would hustle the remaining time along.

She closed the door and made her way back to the nursing station where Courtney was sitting.

Amanda settled once more in her chair, shifting the mouse to bring the computer screen to life. All was quiet in Ward Three at Serenity Lodge.

Even the dark shape hovering in the corner next to Carmel's bed was quiet, watching the old lady's chest rise and fall... waiting.

TWO

Four days off starting tomorrow. I can't wait." Courtney stood up and stretched like a cat. The grin she shot Amanda was also feline, as she pulled her hair back into a ponytail.

Amanda rolled her eyes and finished entering the final words of her report. "Any plans?" Probably nothing like what Amanda would face when the turn-around and four-day reprieve happened to her. She was barely able to get caught up on laundry during that mini-holiday.

"Sleep, baby. That's in between movies on the sofa with Whiskers, and maybe some wine and pizza. Let's face it, there's not a whole lot happening in this town. Thank God for Netflix." Courtney grabbed the key to the medicine cabinet beside the desk and unlocked it. She stood while she did the inventory of medications. If one thing was out of order or missing, she would pick up on that in a heartbeat. It was part of what made her the conscientious nurse whom Amanda respected. "We might need to replenish some of these supplies from the med room, hon." she said.

Amanda ran her hand through her wavy, shoulder-length hair. "The med room's on the other end of the building, and we're both beat to a snot. Make a note and have the day shift do it."

"Sounds like a plan," Courtney shut and locked the box. "They have twice the staff on days anyway." She flopped back into her workstation and made the notes. "You're back tonight, right?"

"Two more shifts for me—if I can survive two nights with Linda, that is." Amanda handed the meds chart to Courtney and sighed. "I don't know what I ever did to make her hate me so much. All the other women here are great to work with."

Courtney's mouth pulled to the side as she gazed at her friend. "She feels threatened by you, Amanda. I mean you worked in the E.R. at Mount Sinai for four years. You're young, sharp as a tack, while she's kind of washed up." She grabbed a bottle of Vicodin and poured a couple into each of the three white paper cups lined up on the tray. "Plus, she knows you're going to try for the supervisor's job when Liz retires. She was a shoo-in for that job before you showed up and expressed an interest."

Amanda rose to help Courtney with the meds, cross checking the chart with what was being doled into the med cups. "As you know, that job is part of the reason that I came here, Courtney. I just wish you'd warned me that I'd be doing battle with the dragon lady to get it."

Courtney laughed, "You would be so much better at being a supervisor. Plus, it pays more and with Will..." The smile dropped. "You know with him getting sick and all, you could use the extra money."

The corner of Amanda's mouth rose. "Not to mention Kelly. When she turned thirteen, it was like she morphed into a butterfly. Now she needs an entire wardrobe change?" Amanda fell silent for a moment. Her daughter was thirteen but it was as though she'd turned seventeen, wearing make-up and an attitude. And forget the kids she was starting to hang out with. If she got that supervisor's job, it would be straight days with more time to get the kid back in line.

"Come on. Don't you remember becoming a teenager? Yeah, okay things were different back then with not so much social media and all the bullshit *that* entails, but..."

Amanda stayed silent. Courtney was only thirty-one, a few years younger, but they were eons apart in how they'd been raised. Courtney was from the classic middle-class family, replete with family vacations to Disneyland and even camping. Amanda had survived her teenage years in *spite* of her parents.

The call button buzzed, yanking Amanda from her past. She glanced over at the desk. It was room eleven...again. What now?

"I'll do a second check on the meds when I get back. I'd better go see what's up with Carmel. Maybe she had another nightmare."

Despite her efforts to be quiet as she hurried, Amanda's sneakers squeaked on the polished floor. It was still way too early for the residents to be disturbed from sleep to start their day. Jane was going to be a real witch if Carmel woke her up again.

When she entered the room all the lights were blazing overhead. Carmel was standing in the small space between Jane's bed and the window. Jane was still asleep snoring loudly despite the brightness of the room, unaware that Carmel stood glaring down at her.

Amanda rushed over and put her arm around the old woman's shoulders. Her hand felt the woman's bones through the thin nightgown as she ushered her away from Jane's space. "Come on Carmel" she whispered. "Was there something you needed? You should be asleep."

The old lady's eyes were dark as a crow's peering at Amanda. "I can't stay here. You must call me a taxi to take me home. I don't know that woman. What kind of hotel is this, where you put a stranger in with me? I'd like to speak with the manager, if you don't mind."

Amanda eased her arm around the old lady, steering her over to her own bed. "Carmel, you're at a nursing home. Dr. Stone...you remember him, don't you? Your home is gone. It burned down." She avoided adding that it was Carmel's negligence which had destroyed it—leaving a pot on the stove while wandering off to the store.

Carmel gaped up at Amanda, as though she was speaking a foreign language. "What? Who are you? Of course I know

Ryan Stone! Please call him for me. I need to get home right now. Ryan will take me home. You tell him Carmel Turner is asking."

Amanda took a deep breath. "I'll speak to Dr. Stone later, I promise. But for now let's get you settled again. Try to get a couple more hours of sleep." The sleeping meds should still be working but obviously Carmel was too distraught. She straightened the old lady's sheets and plumped her pillow before helping her get onto the bed.

Carmel lay back, staring hard at Amanda. "What is your name? I'll need to speak to Ryan about this. You're trying to be kind, I know that. He'll put in a good word with the management for you."

It was hard not to sneer. Of all the people to 'put in a good word' Ryan Stone would be the last person to do that. But it wouldn't hurt to look into what meds he had prescribed for Carmel. Had he referred her to a shrink to see if there were emotional factors contributing to her memory lapses? They obviously had some kind of history together.

"Thanks, Carmel. That's kind of you. My name is Amanda by the way. Would you like me to stay for a little while till you nod off again?"

"No. I'll be fine as soon as Dr. Stone gets here. Maybe I will catnap for a bit till he arrives. You may go." Carmel closed her eyes and rolled over onto her side.

Amanda lifted the blanket higher on Carmel's shoulder and then stepped away from the bed. As she was passing the bathroom in the room she noticed the fluorescent light flickering. Flipping the switch, she made a mental note to mention to Maintenance that the bulb in that room should be changed or adjusted.

She jerked back, covering her nose at a foul smell that drifted in the air around her. It hadn't been there before when she first entered room eleven. She turned the bathroom light back on, deciding to check it. It wouldn't be the first time that a resident had used the toilet without flushing. But when she entered everything was pristine, right down to the tiled blue floor. Odd.

Casting a quick look at the beds and their occupants, she decided one of them must be suffering from gas, fouling the air. She wrinkled her nose at the odor. That was part of the glamorous life as a nurse, right? She shook her head ruefully as she headed to the door.

She left the room, walking quickly to the nursing station to help Courtney with the meds. Some of the drugs were Phenobarbitals, and a second set of eyes prevented any errors or theft.

Courtney's head shot up as she saw Amanda leaving room eleven and heading back to the nursing station. "What are you doing?" she asked.

Amanda shrugged. "Settling Carmel in again." She pointed at the call button display and flicked off the blinking light.

Like a confused barnyard chicken, Courtney's head turned from Amanda to the corridor, and back again. "Yeah, but..."

"But what?"

Courtney gave her head a small shake. "Nothing, I guess. I'm overtired."

Amanda came around the counter. "What?"

A small laugh erupted from Courtney's throat. "It's nothing. I thought I saw you come out of the room a few minutes ago and head down the corridor, is all. I was working on the charts and thought I saw that from the corner of my eye. I figured you were checking the other residents or something." She sat back in her chair and stretched, yawning. "So when you came out just now, it threw me."

Amanda plopped into the chair beside her. "Nope, I was in Carmel's room the whole time."

Courtney shrugged. "No biggie. I didn't even look up completely when it happened, just a side view." She tapped the monitor screen before her. "I was trying to get all the shift notes in." She yawned again. "Oh man, do I need a good night's sleep."

THREE

When Amanda arrived home that morning, it was a little before nine. She tossed her keys on the stand by the door and wandered into the kitchen. Her husband, Will was still in his pajama bottoms and T-shirt sitting at the table having breakfast, but at least he was up. That was a positive sign considering how tired he'd been lately.

He turned and a smile lit up his face. "Hey! How was work? Anything exciting happen?" There were bags under his eyes and a few days of beard growth bristled his jaw.

She stepped over to him and ran a hand along his cheek. "Nothing exciting. There's a new patient who kept me busy for a while. First night, disoriented, nightmares. She thought she was in a hotel the second time I went in." Walking over to the fridge, she plucked the carton of orange juice from the shelf. "Did Kelly get off to school okay?"

"Yeah, although she nearly missed the bus. Again. She spends too much time getting ready. It's grade seven, not the Academy Awards." Will picked up his empty bowl and coffee mug before trudging to the sink to set them there.

On auto-pilot, Amanda plucked the items out and stacked them in the dishwasher. How many times since Will had become ill from chronic fatigue had he walked by the dishwasher to dump his dishes, leaving her to pick up after him? One thing at a time, though. First he had to get better - if he ever got better.

She shook her head. No. He would get better. They'd be a family like they always had been. Maybe even better if... she tried not to dwell on the next thought. Her biological clock was ticking, and if they were ever going to have a second child, it had better be soon. Despite the set-back in Will's health, she wasn't willing to give up on that dream...not yet.

"What are your plans for the day?" She folded her arms over her chest looking up at him. "Are you seeing the doctor?"

He looked away for a moment and sighed. "Look, honey, I know this isn't easy on you. I appreciate all that you do, taking on any extra shifts and keeping the house looking nice. I'm trying. Really I am. The doctor said I should try to get into a regular routine, walking and getting out, rather than moping around. I thought I'd try to go as far as the library today. Maybe tomorrow I'll make it to the park."

Amanda felt the weight of guilt settle on her shoulders. It wasn't his fault he was sick. He was taking his meds and really trying. She'd have to be patient. She went over and put her arms around his muscled torso. Years of muscle built from working in construction, putting in twelve hour days, seven days a week when needed. He wasn't lazy. This was a medical condition.

"I know. I think you should do what the doctor ordered but don't overtire yourself, okay?" She looked up into his dark eyes, seeing the man she had fallen in love with. He was the same guy, just stricken with this rotten disease. She also knew that if he overdid it, he could end up in bed for days, which wouldn't help his mental state, either.

Will let out a long sigh into her hair, pulling her closer. "I'll stop and rest if I get tired. Hell, I'll call a cab to get home if I have to." He kissed her forehead, "But you must be pretty exhausted right now. I'll just change, and then I promise I'll be out of your hair to let you sleep. I promise to be here when Kelly gets home, so that she doesn't wake you."

She squeezed his hand and led the way into the bedroom. As she changed out of her scrubs, she could hear the spray of the shower from the adjoining bathroom. She got into bed and picked up a book to read. There was no way she was going to sleep without giving him a kiss before he started his day.

Fighting sleep, she looked up when he emerged from the bathroom. He was freshly shaved and for a change, he was in beige Dockers instead of the torn blue jeans he normally sported. He'd even chosen a crisp button-down shirt. "You look nice." She set the book down and propped herself up higher.

"Thanks. You know what they say. Fake it till you make it." He stepped over and planted a quick kiss on her forehead. "I'm off now to let you get some sleep. And don't worry about me. I'll take it easy, but the important thing is to keep moving. I'm going to beat this thing, Amanda."

She nodded and squeezed his hand. "I know you will. Wake me at 4 pm so I can see you guys for a while before I go to work, okay?" She settled back into the bed watching him as he closed the blinds to dim the room. This new therapy program had improved Will's outlook and had him moving around, rather than being overmedicated and lying around the house all day. And it would provide contact with people to get him out of his shell.

She closed her eyes when the bedroom door closed. She'd better get some rest. It was hard enough getting through a night shift, but doing it with Linda was a total drag. The one saving grace was the quiet. That is, if the new patient, Carmel got settled in. God help the poor woman if she acted up when Linda was on night duty. She'd know nightmares then, for real. Linda's bedside manner was more like a warden than a nurse sometimes; especially on the overnight shift.

FOUR

Amanda watched the nurses and aides from the day shift leave the floor. She turned to her computer screen to review the notes they'd written about the patients that day. Sometimes when staff rotated off, the odd change in meds or behavior failed to make it into their crossover meetings. It was a routine procedure that was preferable to engaging in forced congeniality with Linda.

From the corner of her eye she could see the stout, fifty-year-old battleaxe employing the same devotion to detail. It was probably the only thing the two of them had in common.

Amanda sat there feeling the lack of chit chat; the silence between the two of them seemed to press down like a dead weight. Before she could come up with something casual to say, Linda's nasal voice broke the silence. "I see the new patient, Carmel Turner, is requesting that Jane be moved from the room. I haven't met her yet, but I'd say she has a snowball's chance in hell of that happening."

Amanda hadn't gotten that far in the report. Linda had settled in at the nurse's station while she had been gabbing with Lilith Granger about her new grandchild. Well, to be accurate, Lilith had done most of the talking, even showing pictures of her first granddaughter.

She scanned down to the entries on Carmel, commenting absently, "Carmel had a bad first night yesterday, with nightmares." She read the other entry. Dr. Stone had been in and examined Carmel. *'Vitals normal, increasing the Lorazepam dosage to ten mgs PRN. Periodical lapses into dementia , which considering her age is to be expected.'*

Her eyes narrowed. No mention of a referral for psychiatric evaluation. Considering that the woman lived alone with no living relative or visible means of support, depression could be a factor in the onset of dementia. True, she was in her seventies, but isolation often led to a deterioration in mental acuity.

She looked over at Linda. "It's probably better for Carmel's sake to be in a double room. It might help to keep her grounded and lucid, especially if Jane is her roommate."

That was one good thing about Jane Drogan. She was a former high school teacher who called a spade a spade. She'd probably seen all the hijinks there were and could stop them with a word. Underneath the stern exterior, though, Jane was a caring person— except when waking her in the middle of the night.

Linda rose and adjusted the waistline of her scrub pants over her generous middle. "It's time to round up the herd. I'll do the recreation room if you do the sunroom. I'm sure the kitchen staff will be eager to get home after evening snacks are done."

Amanda decided to ignore Linda's remark likening the patients to a 'herd'. Linda had worked there for so long that she didn't even see that comparing the elderly to docile cattle was demeaning. With any luck, she'd make a slip like that in the interview, and it would be a strike against her. Or at least it would be if Dr. Stone wasn't on the hiring board. The man was so dull, he'd never pick up on it.

She clicked the mouse, locking the computer, and stood up.

"What do you think of Dr. Stone? From what I hear, he's here more than his predecessor ever was. That guy did this on the side with his own practice taking precedence. Stone's here practically full-time."

"If the new owners are happy, then does it matter what we think?"

'Gotcha', Amanda thought. She stared at the older woman. "It matters a lot what we think, Linda. I'm a nurse—"

"As am I, dear."

Amanda bridled internally. She hated Linda using that term 'dear'. It was so condescending! She held up her hand like a traffic cop as she replied, "Yes, you are. But you don't find it curious about Dr. Stone's hours? How is he able to support himself on what they pay him here?"

Linda smiled and shook her head slowly with a patronizing smile. "I don't have the slightest idea what the owners are paying Dr. Stone; it's none of my business, hon." She darted a finger at Amanda. "Nor is it yours."

"Yeah, but—"

Linda cut her off with a sharp wave of her hand. "But nothing, dear." She pointed her thumb behind her down the corridor. "Look at the results he's had with the zombies in Ward Two! All the clients there—and we call them 'clients', not 'patients' Amanda— went from being either bed-ridden or zonked out in chairs all day, to being completely ambulatory, since Dr. Stone started attending them." She folded her arms and peered down her nose at Amanda. "That's something positive. Or didn't you notice?"

Amanda felt her face grow warm and she looked away.

Before she could formulate a reply, Linda delivered the coup de grace. "Now, if you don't mind, could you stop gossiping about other staff members and do your job?"

Amanda turned back to see Linda heading down the hall. There was even a saunter in the sway of her haunches, relishing her snide comment. The bitch. Amanda's eyes narrowed as she continued going into the part of the wing where the sunroom was housed.

The last glimmer of a blood-red sunset on the horizon flowed through a wall of windows. A group of women sat around a table playing bridge while Jane and Myrtle Braden, the two former teachers, played Scrabble at the other end of the room. Three other residents sat alone reading. They had unplugged from the mindless drivel of sitcoms where the TV in the recreation room dominated. They also tended to retire a bit later. She'd come back for them in another hour or so.

She smiled as she approached the bridge players. "Five-minute warning, ladies. It's eight forty-five." When Mable, an elderly woman with an oxygen tube taped under her nose, peered up at her, Amanda added, "I'll give you a hand getting back to your room, Mable."

Giving another patient's shoulder a little squeeze, she chirped, "Tally up, ladies. Tomorrow's another day for your game." When the two women on the winning team groaned, she shrugged and continued to over to where the Scrabble board was set up. "Who's ahead here?"

Jane looked up before setting four tiles on the board, making the word 'quilt', using a stray 't' opening. "That's thirty-four points right there. I'd say I just won."

"For this time, Jane." Myrtle finished tallying up the score and tossed her remaining tile in the box. "I'll clean your clock tomorrow night." She rose to her feet, and with a disgruntled huff, she walked away.

Amanda winked at Jane and whispered, "Sore loser, huh?"

Jane's eyebrows bobbed high, "And she tries to cheat!" She tapped the dictionary that sat on the table. "This baby keeps her honest though." The smile dropped from her face when she looked up at Amanda. "Is that new one going to keep me awake all night again? I swear if she starts screaming, I'll put a pillow over her face."

"Don't do that, Jane. I'd miss you when they drag you off to prison." She grinned. If Jane only knew. Carmel had her own set of complaints about Jane's snoring.

She looked over at the women reading, but none of them were making any sign that they were ready to go. That was normal for them. They'd probably been night owls all their lives, so their patterns of sleep hadn't changed.

Mable sat in her wheelchair while the other three women made their way to the door. Amanda stepped in behind her and toed the brake off, making sure that the oxygen tank was securely in place before pushing the handles. "You really like bridge, Mable. I never learned the game. Maybe one day you can teach me."

"I'd like that." The words wheezed out from the old woman's throat. She turned her head to flash a grin up at Amanda.

Back at the nurses' station, the call signal for room eleven was blinking steadily. There was no sign of Linda anywhere nearby, so Amanda walked down to check what the problem was. She wasn't even halfway down the corridor when she heard the heated argument coming from room eleven.

"You're not staying here in my room!" Carmel snarled.

"It's not your room! I was here first! If anyone should leave, it should be you!"

Uh-oh. That was Jane. Her booming bellow overwhelmed Carmel's voice by a mile.

Amanda rushed in, closing the door behind her. "Enough, both of you!" Carmel sat on the edge of the bed, her mouth a tight line while she glared at Amanda and Jane. Jane never wavered, hands on sturdy hips, defying Carmel with an icy stare.

Carmel turned from Jane, stretching a bony hand out to Amanda. Her eyes welled with tears while her shoulders drooped. "Please. Dr. Stone told me I would have a room of my own. I can't sleep with that cow snoring and smacking her lips continually. I had a horrible night last night."

"Cow! Who are you calling cow?"

Carmel shot a withering look at Jane, "Okay, bovine, if you'd prefer."

Amanda felt like a referee when she stepped between them. "Stop. There'll be no name calling anymore. We treat each other with respect here." She looked at Carmel, "There was no note in the chart to change your room." Not that it was ever going to happen, anyway. The only available bed was the one closest to the nursing station reserved for patients who required more intensive medical care.

"Great." Jane flopped down on her bed, turning her back to them.

Carmel sniffed, wiping the tear from her cheek. "There must be some mistake. I can't stay here anymore. Where are my clothes?"

Amanda sunk down next to the old woman. "Give it another night, Carmel. If you have trouble sleeping, I can get you some earplugs." She tapped Carmel's hand. "Do you normally have a snack or drink before bed? I'll see what we can get you to make this more pleasant. But you have to stay here. Sorry."

"I don't want any of your snacks. I want to go home." Her eyes narrowed and she folded her hands together on her lap, in a classic pout.

Amanda rose, "I'll see that you get some warmed milk when food services comes around. That might help you sleep." She looked down at the old woman who now wrung her hands, staring hard at her lap. The woman's defeat touched a nerve. "I'm here to help you, Carmel. I'm a nurse, not a jailor." When she received no response, she tried another tack. "Do you have any hobbies? Do you knit or read, do crosswords? Personally, I like to sketch. Whatever you want. I can help with whatever interests you."

Carmel looked up and her eyes bored into Amanda's as a small smile twitched her lips. Her eyes drilled into Amanda with deliberate precision as she spoke. "No. Whatever I need or would like is beyond you."

Amanda's head snapped back like she'd just been slapped. *'Beyond you'*. Memories of her mother using that same term, in an identical tone of voice, flooded over her. *'Don't try to be a pretty girl, Amanda; that's beyond you.'* She felt her heart begin to beat faster as she watched the woman's eyes and heard her mother's words echo in her mind. *'Stop studying so much, math is beyond you.'*

Amanda closed her eyes for a moment to banish long-past memories and opened them again to look at Carmel. The woman watched her closely, the small smile now...smug?

But that was crazy. Carmel was just an addled old woman. Amanda gathered her wits and forced a lightness in her voice that she definitely didn't feel. "Okay then. But if you want to just visit, or talk about anything, I'm here."

She looked over at Jane who was making a show of rummaging in her dresser, not eavesdropping—which of course she was.

When Jane, nightgown and housecoat in hand, went past them to go to the bathroom to change, Amanda continued. "I know that you lived alone, but surely you must have friends or even a distant relative whom we could contact. A visit from a friend might cheer you up."

Carmel shook her head. The silver hair was like spun sugar falling almost to her shoulders. "No. I lived a solitary life. I always enjoyed my privacy..." She glanced over at Jane's empty bed. "...which is why I can't have that woman in this room with me."

Amanda was silent, gazing at the old lady. There were only a handful of private rooms but they were currently occupied, with a long waiting list. "Just give it some more time, Carmel. Try to keep an open mind. You don't have to be best friends with Jane but at least be polite. I'm sure she'll return the favor."

When Jane came out of the bathroom, her purple housecoat tucked neatly around her, the stern look in her eyes was anything but forgiving.

Amanda tried to calm the troubled waters one last time. "Do you play Scrabble, Carmel? Jane claims to be the champion here at Serenity. Maybe you could challenge her."

Jane shot a dark look at Amanda before commenting. "Any time. Any place." She shook her head. "Actually, it would have to be in the sunroom. That is, if she's brave enough to venture out of here."

Amanda looked down at Carmel. "You didn't leave your room today? I mean, aside from seeing Dr. Stone?"

Carmel's silence was the answer. She looked up at Amanda and her eyes narrowed. "I hate this room and I hate this place. It's a bad place."

There was no placating Carmel at this point. Amanda looked over at Jane who was getting settled in her bed. She placed her hand on Carmel's shoulder and gave it a small squeeze, "I'll be around later with sleeping meds."

When she opened the door to leave the room, she almost stepped into Linda. Immediately the older woman jerked back. She showed no embarrassment for eavesdropping and didn't miss a beat in commenting, "I've seen this kind of whiney behavior from a new resident more than a few times. She'll get past it faster if there's no audience to play to. For Carmel's own good, don't coddle her, dear."

Amanda's eyes grew wider and her back stiffened at Linda's criticism. She tried mentally counting to ten but didn't make it past three before the words burst forth. "I'm not coddling her. It's called listening and trying to be empathetic. It's part of what makes a good nurse. You should try it sometime."

She darted around Linda and strode down the hallway. Behind her, Linda countered, "I was nursing when you were still a youngster playing hopscotch, little girl."

Amanda's jaw tightened when she noticed the food service worker, Janis Baines, standing next to her trolley, her gaze ping-ponging between Linda and Amanda. It was bad enough to be bickering with the older nurse, but for the scene to be witnessed by other workers was downright embarrassing. She swallowed hard and then spoke softly to Janis, "Please see that Carmel in room 11 has warm milk with her snack."

Janis nodded but placed her hand on Amanda's arm, stopping her. "Is everything all right?"

Great. Amanda smiled though she knew that the little spat she'd had with Linda would be all over the place the next day. Janis was nice, but she was a total gossip. "Yes. Linda and I had a slight difference of opinion. That's all." She shrugged and slipped away to the nurse's station.

After clicking the computer's mouse and bringing the nursing records up on the screen, Amanda focused all of her attention on it. Even so, from the edge of her vision, she saw that Linda was coming up the hall to join her. It was a relief to answer when the call light from room twelve lit up.

As she passed by Linda, her words were curt, "Mable is ready to go to bed now. I'll look after her." She held her tongue, not adding the rest of the words she was thinking: *'...better than you could ever hope to.'*

It was going to be a long night.

Amanda didn't know the half of it.

If you enjoyed this free sample, you'll love the rest of Graveyard Shift available exclusively on Amazon!

Made in the
USA
Middletown, DE

76402527R00125